Also by Candy Denman

THE DR CALLIE HUGHES
CRIME SCENE INVESTIGATIONS
Book 1: Dead Pretty
Book 2: Body Heat
Book 3: Guilty Party
Book 4: Vital Signs
Book 5: Deadly Remedies
Book 6: Murder Lust
Book 7: Bones of Contention
Book 8: Hanging Question

STANDALONE
Deadly Treatment

DEADLY TREATMENT

CANDY DENMAN

THE BOOK FOLKS

Revised edition 2025
The Books Folks
A Joffe Books Company
www.thebookfolks.com

First published by The Malvern Publishing Company
in Great Britain in 1987

ISBN: 978-1-80462-348-0

A Note to the Reader

Please note this book is from the 1980s, a time before smartphones and ubiquitous CCTV, when social attitudes were very different.

For Bob,
with special thanks to Maisie.

Chapter 1

The young man looked around the cold, bare room and shuddered, more with excitement than horror. The walls were covered with white tiles, between which the grouting showed grey and decayed. There were two glass cupboards full of steel instruments, but the only other furniture was an assortment of trolleys and a large, moveable operating-theatre light.

"I don't know how Jim can work down here, day in and day out, with nothing but corpses for company. It's unnatural." He paused to watch what the older man was doing, and then continued in a more cheerful voice, "They say he's a bit touched, talks to them and sometimes sings them lullabies." Getting no response, he turned back to the particular cadaver they were dealing with that morning. "The coroner didn't mind us doing the post-mortem then?"

"No, not at all," Dr Geoffrey Hull grunted as he set to work splitting the sternum down the middle. For a few moments the only sound was that of the small electric saw he was using. "In fact, he was all too happy to let us do it for a change. I mean it's a fairly straightforward case, nothing unusual, and the coroner's usual team are particularly busy at the moment." He peered into the thoracic cavity. "No signs of either cardiomyopathy or cardiomegaly. Doesn't look as though there were any chronic heart problems. Right, let's take it out and open it up. My bet is that we find a massive thrombus in the coronary artery."

His assistant watched as the senior pathologist deftly removed the heart and lungs in one piece and placed them on a dissecting tray. He opened the heart, starting at the aortic arch and cutting through into the atria.

"That's odd!" Hull stared fixedly at the heart's interior and then quickly slit open the pulmonary artery.

"Some air must have got in when you dissected it out."

"Don't be stupid. Look at the way the blood has clotted around the air bubbles. They've been there some considerable time. In fact, I think they must be the cause of death." He extended the slit in the artery a little further to expose even more bubbles.

"Christ, it can't be an air embolus, can it?"

"It can," Hull answered quietly. "And it is. A massive one. I think perhaps we should get in touch with the coroner's office and get their advice. It's not every day you come across something like this. I'll go and phone them. You stay where you are. Don't touch anything and don't talk to anyone, either."

For a moment they both stared at the mutilated cadaver. The young doctor seemed shocked at the full implications of their find.

"You don't think this is a case of negligence or incompetence, do you?"

"I don't know, but the only alternative is murder, which isn't very nice either," Hull said grimly as he reached for the telephone. "Hullo, switchboard? Outside line, please."

* * *

"What exactly is the problem?" asked the Home Office pathologist as soon as he arrived.

"Here, you can see for yourself. Gas bubbles in the right atrium, ventricle and the pulmonary artery. We also found some here, in a few of the smaller vessels of the brain, which we looked at after I telephoned you, but there aren't many, so it must have been pretty quick."

"Fairly conclusive then. Any idea how the gas got into the circulation?"

"I opened up the vein where his intravenous infusion was situated and there were several large bubbles there, so the suggestion is that a considerable volume of gas, probably air, entered the bloodstream via the intravenous infusion. I would guess that at the very least twenty millilitres must have got in, and that's one hell of a lot for an accident. Death would have been instantaneous from that much, but immediately after death more air would seem to have been injected to make sure. I can't absolutely rule out any hospital responsibility, but we may well be talking about a total of fifty mills of air, taking into account the fact that a large amount would have dissolved in the bloodstream and some might have been absorbed into the tissues."

"It sounds like probable homicide. We'll have to do more tests of course, check the gas levels in the blood surrounding the bubbles as opposed to elsewhere, but I'm sure you're right about the amounts and that makes any other conclusion unlikely. If you could arrange an internal hospital inquiry, I'll sort out the tests, make a preliminary report to the police and take a look for anything else of interest. Do you mind if we work here or shall I arrange for everything to be moved?" He waved his hand vaguely in the direction of the corpse.

"No, no. Do carry on here. Just let us know if you need anything." Hull left the pathologist and his team to their work while he and his assistant went to alert the dean to the problem.

* * *

Sergeant "Hoppy" Hopwood looked up as Detective Inspector Bright entered the room, sauntered up to his desk and shuffled through the papers in his tray.

The CID offices had been partially modernised ten years earlier, but the decorating had never been completed. At the time, the idea had been to make the main office area open plan, with desks tucked in cubby holes created by moveable screens. In practice, the screens had got in the way and were moved around so much that they soon broke and had long since been removed. Much of the furniture was old and ill-suited to modern technology. There were not enough desks to go around, so the telephones often ended up on the floor when two people were using a space intended for only one.

"What's happened while we were at lunch?" Bright asked cheerfully of nobody in particular. "Who has been murdered and by whom?" He was proud of his ability to speak "proper" English, but always lapsed into his native tongue before long, making it obvious that he hailed from somewhere around the Bow Bells.

He picked up an incident report. "Oh God, not another burglary! And a real amateur job by the sound of it. The ruddy door kicked down, in broad daylight, and nobody saw or heard anything. Typical!" He shook his head in despair.

"I've put Johnson and Dingwall on to it, not that they'll find anything helpful," Hoppy told him.

"Always the optimist, Hoppy, aren't you? Now, I'd better catch up on some of this paperwork before we're all buried under it."

He sat down and opened the top file while Hoppy answered a telephone that was persistently ringing at another desk.

"Bright!" Detective Chief Superintendent Willard shouted through the door and continued down the corridor to his own office with Bright in hot pursuit.

When Bright returned, there was an air of urgency about him.

"Hoppy, I want you to get everyone you can in here. I'm off to find Sergeant Harper. She'll be setting up an incident room in the lecture hall, so if you send everyone in there pronto, I'll be along to brief them in a minute or six," he said and rushed off.

"Smith," Hoppy called. "Go to the canteen and get Slim. Use force if necessary, but get him into the lecture hall."

Temporary Detective Constable Smith had been laboriously filling in forms most of the morning and jumped at the chance of doing something different. As he left, Hoppy picked up the telephone and began to call all the off-duty CID staff.

Sergeant Harper was already busy arranging extra telephone lines, computer link-ups, vast amounts of paper and forms, and borrowing staff from other stations when Bright arrived at the lecture hall. Inside were the ten people Hoppy had managed to find. Three were detective constables, Johnson and Dingwall having returned from their burglary investigation; two were temporary detective constables; four were uniformed constables, one female; and another was a scene-of-crime officer.

Bright sipped the plastic cup of tea he had fetched from the station machine and grimaced. He put it down hurriedly and began the briefing.

"Sir Edward Ellis died in hospital last night and this morning's post-mortem showed suspicious findings. It's not definitely homicide yet and we probably won't even have the full report until tomorrow. Meanwhile, the scene of the alleged crime will have been disinfected and a new patient put in the bed before Sir Edward was even cold. No fingerprints, footprints, or particles of dust will have been left after the cleaners have been – so your Sherlock technique will be of no use at all," he said to the scene-of-crime officer.

"I want Sergeants Hopwood, Smith, Slim and two uniforms – you two will do," he pointed to the WPC and an older-than-average constable, "to go to the hospital with the SOC officer. I want initial-action statements from everyone in the same block at the hospital, all the staff on duty last night, cleaners, visitors and anyone else you can think of; Sergeant Harper will send reinforcements as soon as they arrive. Oh, and by the way, we want this kept quiet." He paused for a moment to let this sink in. "That may seem impossible, but we don't want the press breathing down our necks at this stage. I suggest you tell everyone you are investigating some thefts from staff and patients or something. You sort out the story, Hoppy, and I don't want anyone using their radios either. There's always someone listening who didn't ought to, so only normal messages, please. Right, off you go." He dismissed them and turned to the remaining five.

"Johnson, you and one uniformed constable come with me to the family house. Which leaves Dingwall with Temporary DC Greaves and the last uniformed constable to stay here and help Sergeant Harper get everything organised. Dingwall, I want all the information you can get on Sir Edward and his family – you know, check *Who's Who, intel* and the files, though I doubt we'll have anything on them apart from unpaid parking tickets. And see if you can get any info on the hospital: plans, recent problems, crime reports on intruders and the like. You'd better let Chelsea station know what's going on as Sir Edward lived on their patch. If the story breaks, they'll need to keep the press from the door, but meanwhile it would be good if they could just keep a low-profile watch on things. Oh, and I'd like at least six more people doing initial actions at the hospital by lunchtime. C'mon, you two," he finished, picked up his jacket and left.

* * *

"Now, no one is to be frightened. We have just called you here this morning to tell us all you know about Sir Edward Ellis's death. Nobody is accusing any of you of making a mistake or being careless. We just want to clear things up a little because, as I'm sure you will have heard, the post-mortem showed that some things were not altogether normal."

Professor John Gallagher was an elderly man who had been dean of St Bede's for several years. He had a kindly manner and spoke to everyone as though he or she were a child. He didn't mean to be patronising; it was just that he was in the habit of speaking to children. He had been a paediatric consultant for twenty-five years and had raised six children of his own.

"We've decided that everyone should come in at once, and we will just have a little discussion of the events, rather than anything so grand as an inquiry." He turned and entered the room. If any blame could possibly be attached to the hospital or any members of staff, there would have to be a formal inquiry, with all the governors and heads of departments, but for the moment this was all that was necessary or desirable. He wanted to attract as little interest in the proceedings as possible.

He paused in the doorway and looked with dismay at the row of people seated behind the long, polished oak table, with their pencils, paper, and glasses of water. They looked very intimidating. All of them felt they had to be there, to protect someone else's interests no doubt. None of them would admit to curiosity, probably not even to themselves. The group behind the table consisted of the senior nursing officer for the surgical block, the principal nursing officer, a senior consultant surgeon (not involved in the case), the hospital administrator and the senior pathologist, Dr Geoffrey Hull. The sub-dean and the dean himself reluctantly joined them. Everyone connected with Sir Edward's care then came and sat in a semi-circle in front of the table. The dean looked worriedly at the two young student nurses who had been on night duty. Understandably, they looked very pale, tired, and more than a little frightened.

"I realise that Sir Edward's case history probably has little relevance here, but I would be grateful if you could just run over it briefly for us, Mr O'Neill," the dean said to the consultant surgeon in charge of the case.

Mr O'Neill glanced at the notes which he had brought in with him and was about to speak when there was a knock at the door. A nursing officer poked her head into the room and said that there was a policeman outside who wondered if they would mind him sitting in.

"Really, I must protest!" said O'Neill. "This is a private inquiry and we shall all feel less able to speak frankly if there is a policeman taking notes in the background."

"Excuse me, sir," said Hopwood, sneaking in behind the nursing officer. "I won't be taking notes at this stage, and it will make things much easier when I have to question you individually and take statements. It's just to give me a little background knowledge, so to speak." Hopwood had the advantage of looking like a solid and dependable village policeman. He glanced around the room, hoping to muster some support. One of the younger nurses was looking horrified, but most of the others just appeared doubtful. Hoppy knew that no one would want an outsider to know if there was a suggestion that anyone had acted incorrectly, but they would also be concerned that it did not look as if they were trying to hush it all up.

"I don't see why the officer should not be present at this informal meeting. We are merely seeking to unearth a few facts and if it will be of use to the police, I feel we should be glad to help." It was Dr Hull who had spoken in Hoppy's favour.

"I agree," the principal nursing officer said. "I, for one, do not believe that anyone here is in any way to blame. I am certain that a hideous crime has been committed, and we must none of us rest until the culprit has been found."

While Hoppy felt that she was taking things a bit far, he was not going to argue with someone who looked like a formidable and overweight pug. Looking round the rest of the room, he realised that nobody else was going to take issue with her either.

"Well, I think that is agreed then," the dean said quickly before there could be any disagreement. "Do come in and take seat, Officer. Or is it Sergeant?" He looked questioningly at Hoppy.

"Yes, sir. Sergeant Hopwood."

"Oh, thank you. Yes, well, Sergeant, make yourself comfortable."

Hoppy took the chair indicated and placed it in the corner, a little behind the table group and well to the side. He hoped he might be forgotten there but he would still be able to see the faces of all those giving statements.

"Let's start with you again, George," the dean said when everybody had settled down.

"If I must." O'Neill was not happy about the uninvited witness, and began by pointedly introducing himself to Hoppy, before continuing, "Sir Edward first presented in Casualty at 21.15 on Sunday. He was seen there by my registrar, Mr Kirkly." He nodded in the direction of a man who was busy inspecting his fingernails.

"Mr Kirkly examined Sir Edward and diagnosed intestinal obstruction. He contacted me at home and I came in straight away. I joined them in the theatre. Dr Dixon was the anaesthetist" – a thin anxious man nodded vigorously at this – "and the surgery was plain sailing. We found an area of intussusception in the descending colon." He looked directly at Hoppy and explained, "That is, an area of the bowel that had telescoped in on itself, causing an obstruction. As the area had also strangulated and become gangrenous, we removed it and performed an end-to-end anastomosis."

Again, he stopped and explained pointedly to Hoppy, "We joined the remaining ends of the bowel together. I then left Kirkly to finish closing up and went off to have some coffee. I didn't see Sir Edward again until the next morning, when he was as right as rain, complaining about being on the main ward. I explained that it was so that the nurses could keep an eye on him, but he insisted on a private room at the very least, and that's why he was moved. Sir Edward seemed to feel that his GP should have sent him to a private hospital in the first place, but I explained that they often are unable to deal with acute emergencies. I told him that he would receive excellent care at St Bede's and that he would soon be well enough to transfer to a private hospital. And so he would have been if this had not happened." O'Neill came to an abrupt halt and glared at the people behind the table, daring them to disagree.

"Oh yes, quite," the dean reassured him. "I think we can take it that all went well during the actual operation, or the patient would have died on the table or during the first post-operative night. Now, if we could just go over the events immediately prior to the decease, please." He had a pile of medical notes in front of him and he picked up Sir Edward's drugs chart. "We have it on record here that the patient commenced intravenous antibiotic therapy immediately after the operation, and also started intravenous cimetidine on the night of his death."

"He had been taking cimetidine tablets for some months because of his gastric ulcers, and it was considered important that this treatment be continued. He was taking nothing orally, and this might have caused an acute exacerbation of the ulcers," O'Neill explained.

"Thank you. Now, both drugs were due at 10 p.m.," the Dean continued. "The first drug was ampicillin and, as it had been given before, the night sister gave it and Student Nurse Banks checked it. The first dose of any course of intravenous drugs has to be administered by a doctor, in case of any reaction, but thereafter it can be given by a qualified nurse. All drugs must be checked by two people. As two unqualified nurses were in charge of the ward last night, the night sister on duty came to give the drug," he explained to a grateful Hoppy, who still did not quite understand who was given what or why. He listened carefully while the night sister told them that she and Nurse Banks had both checked the antibiotic and then she had given it with Nurse Banks witnessing. They also administered a painkiller to settle Sir Edward at the same time. All seemed to be in order so far.

The houseman then explained that he had been a little late coming in to give the second injection, of cimetidine, because he had been held up on one of the other wards. He cleared his throat and continued, "I watched the nurse draw it up and then I went into the side room to give it."

"Alone?" queried the principal nursing officer.

"Er, yes, but the nurse did check I went into the right room."

Everyone in the room looked from the uncomfortable young doctor to Nurse Banks, who burst out, "Mr Childs was calling out and one of the other patients was buzzing. My junior had nipped out to the loo, and so I was on my own. I know I'm supposed to watch the doctor give the injection, but Mr Childs was climbing over his cot-sides and he might have fallen and hit his head or something."

The principal nursing officer looked unimpressed at this explanation. "You know that is no excuse, Nurse Banks. You should have asked Dr Cawthorne to wait a moment while you dealt with the situation. I know that junior nurses sometimes find it difficult to ask a doctor to wait, but patient safety must come first. You are a third year now and you should have spoken up. If the doctor refuses to wait, then the nurse can refuse to sign for the injection. We have set procedures to cover all these events, to protect the staff as well as to ensure patient safety. You knew very well what you should do, but failed in your duty. It is just not good enough."

Nurse Banks was busily examining her feet and trying not to cry at this criticism.

The houseman jumped to his feet and almost shouted, "Well, look here, Sir Edward was just fine when I left him. You can't really believe that I would pump air into one of my patients."

"Now, now, Dr Cawthorne. No one is suggesting anything of the sort. We are merely reminding everyone here that there are set procedures to protect both staff and patients. It is rather a pity that you didn't stick to it on this occasion, because then we would all know how things stood. Now both these drugs were due at 10 p.m. The first was given pretty much on time, but the second was given rather later. It is recorded on the fluids chart here that a new bag of intravenous dextrose/saline was apparently put up at a quarter to eleven. The chart has been initialled by the two student nurses. Now, was this put up before, after or between the injections?" the Dean asked and peered over his glasses at the nurses, who were both looking thoughtful.

Nurse Banks was the first to speak. "I'm pretty certain I checked it between drugs, but the last bag wasn't quite through and Nurse Jensen was going to change it when the old bag had finished."

The principal nursing officer tapped her pencil on her notepad and shook her head sternly. The night sister tried to come to Nurse Banks's rescue by saying, "I know that it isn't correct procedure, but it is standard practice, and while I know that doesn't make it right, Nurse Banks had no reason to believe that Nurse Jensen might be incapable of changing a bag herself."

"There is no point in having correct procedures if it is 'standard practice' to ignore them," was the PNO's icy reply.

The dean intervened again. He didn't want tempers to be lost; he just wanted to know the facts. "Yes, well now, Nurse Jensen, perhaps you can enlighten us as to when you changed the bags?"

Nurse Jensen was looking extremely frightened and blurted out, "I don't remember! I can't think straight."

"Well, can you remember if it was before or after you went out to the cloakroom? As we know that the second drug was given while you were there."

"Oh, it was before I went to the toilet, I'm sure."

"Right, well that gets the sequence of events straight." The dean smiled at Nurse Jensen.

"Just one moment!" the houseman resident said indignantly.

"What seems to be the problem, Dr Cawthorne?"

"It must have been saline up when I gave the injection, because I didn't have to flush it through. If the new bag, with dextrose in, had been up, Nurse Banks would have checked and I would have given a saline rinse. I'm sure I looked at the bag to see what was running." Suddenly his face brightened. "Another thing – I remember the bag was nearly empty, so it couldn't have just been put up."

He looked triumphantly across at Nurse Jensen, who in turn scowled and repeated stubbornly, "I put it up before I went to the toilet."

"I even mentioned it to Nurse Banks." Dr Cawthorne seemed desperate to prove his point. "I told her not to forget to put a new bag up as the old one was nearly through." He looked anxiously at Nurse Banks, but she refused to meet his eyes.

"I really don't remember the doctor saying that, but he may have done," she said. "I had a lot on my mind at the time. I know I didn't draw up a saline rinse, but I admit I had forgotten to check." She looked tired and miserable. "If I had watched the doctor give the injection, I'm sure I would have remembered, but we were so busy," she finished lamely.

"This is the way that accidents happen, Nurse. You must learn to keep your head, even under pressure. This is what we train you for, but you are obviously not ready for the responsibilities that we expect you to take. I shall have a word with your tutor about this. If you had been qualified, you might have given the injection and the patient might have developed a blood clot or the drug could have reacted with the dextrose. While other lapses might be considered forgivable, not checking the infusion was definitely negligent."

"I really feel I must take some of the blame," said the night sister, rushing bravely to Nurse Banks's defence. "I should have realised the problems and sent some extra help."

"We, um, don't seem to be getting very far here. Perhaps we could return to the matter of Sir Edward's decease," the dean said, stopping the discussion. "We have been unable to establish the exact time of death, or who was the last person to see Sir Edward alive, but at about ten past midnight Nurse Banks went into the room and found him dead. Is that right?" He looked at Nurse Banks questioningly.

"Yes, that's right. I was just doing a routine look-around. I was checking that everyone was all right and settled for the night. I entered Sir Edward's room and he seemed asleep. He looked very uncomfortable and I went to adjust one of his pillows. As I got nearer, I could see he wasn't breathing. I felt for a pulse, but there wasn't one, so I pulled the emergency buzzer and started to resuscitate him. Nurse Jensen came in and I sent her to make the crash call and get the emergency box. The team arrived, but it was no use."

For Hoppy's benefit, the Dean explained that "crash team" was the name given to the group of doctors and other staff on call for emergency resuscitation. Then he continued, "Well, that seems to be all. We know that every effort was made to resuscitate Sir Edward, but it was to no avail. I think we can say that it is likely that he died sometime between 10.45 p.m. and midnight. This agrees with Dr Hull's findings. So you see, it would be helpful to find out the correct sequence of events. We must find out who was the last person here to see Sir Edward alive." He stared first at Dr Cawthorne and then at Nurse Jensen.

"Oh, but I saw Dr Cawthorne go into the side room at eleven thirty," Nurse Jensen burst out, "much later than the injections and things, and he left a few minutes later, so you see none of that matters." Everyone stared at Nurse Jensen and then at the astonished Dr Cawthorne.

Chapter 2

Bright knocked at the door and, as he heard footsteps approaching, adjusted his jacket and stood up straight, trying to make himself look taller.

"I'm sorry to disturb you, sir," he said in his official business voice when the door opened, "but I am Detective Inspector Bright of the Metropolitan Police and I would like to speak to Mr Richard Ellis."

The tall, thin man who had answered the door, paused for a moment. "Perhaps you had better come in, Inspector," he said. "I am Richard Ellis."

He opened the door wider to allow Bright and his two companions, DC Johnson and the uniformed constable, to enter. They stopped in the spacious hall, Richard seemingly undecided as to where they should go next. With a slight shrug of his shoulders, he ushered them past a heavy oak door into a very masculine room, decorated in the classic and unimaginative study style. Everything was brown and mellow. Over the fireplace there was a dismal old portrait of a dismal old ancestor, and hunting prints covered the wall by the doorway. The leather chairs looked comfortable and the desk well used, but Bright was certain that the leather-bound books covering the remaining walls had never been read.

Richard sat in the chair behind a large and solid-looking desk. He seemed self-conscious about his position but composed himself as Bright and the constables were seated. "Now, perhaps you can tell me what this is all about, Inspector?" he asked.

Irritated by his faintly patronising tone of voice, Bright stuck rigidly to his official language. It made him sound pompous but helped him not to respond to insults and slights, both real and imagined. "We have come here to interview yourself and the other members of Sir Edward Ellis's family as to their movements last night," he said. "The post-mortem on Sir Edward's body has revealed that his death may not have been entirely due to natural causes."

Richard looked at Bright in disbelief and then ran his fingers through his wispy blond hair. "What do you mean, not entirely due to natural causes? I mean, are you suggesting that the surgeon's knife may have slipped? Or that a member of the hospital staff gave him an overdose or something?" He paused for a moment and, seeing Bright's non-committal expression in response to his questions, added in a quieter voice, "Or are you suggesting that my father was murdered?"

Bright hesitated for a second before answering deliberately, "It is a possibility that cannot be ignored, sir."

Richard slumped back in his chair, stunned by this news.

"I'm sorry, Inspector," he said with a slight shake of his head, "It's a bit of a shock suddenly to hear that the police believe your father may have been murdered. I mean, I haven't even really come to terms with the fact that he is dead yet."

"I'm sorry, sir," Bright said in a softer voice, "but I am afraid that I shall have to interview you all."

"I suppose there is no chance that this is all a mistake?" Richard asked hopefully.

"No sir, I'm afraid not."

"Right, well, I'd better go and break the news then." Richard did not move but sat where he was, chewing his lower lip and looking worried. "Oh God," he said despairingly, "if this has been a shock for me, just think what it's going to be like for my stepmother." He ran his fingers through his hair again before standing up. "If you would excuse me, Inspector, I think I should go and talk to the rest of the family for a moment. They are all next door. We came round to be with my stepmother, so that she wouldn't be on her own," he explained.

"Of course, sir," Bright answered and stood up politely as Richard Ellis left the room. He wandered around, looking at the pictures, fiddling with the ornaments and then reading aloud the titles on the books.

"Shakespeare's *Sonnets*. *Silas Marner*. Couldn't even begin to pronounce the next one. *Northanger Abbey*. Something foreign. Oh, look." He stooped towards a pile of more battered-looking books. "Lots of ancient volumes of *Punch*." He flipped through the pages of one, pausing to read the odd bit. "I can't understand why anyone ever found some of these cartoons funny," he said to Johnson, quickly replacing the book as he heard Richard returning.

"My stepmother would like to meet you, Inspector, but wonders if I could phone our solicitors first. Naseby was due to come round later today anyway, but she feels it might be for the best if he were to be here when you interview us."

"It would be helpful for me to speak to your solicitor as well, Mr Ellis, but I am pressed for time, so if he could come as quickly as possible, I would appreciate it."

"Yes, yes, of course." Richard seemed disconcerted that Bright wanted to speak to Naseby, but had no choice but to ring him immediately. Bright listened from the study doorway as Richard used the telephone in the hall.

"He's on his way," Richard said when he had finished. "So, if you come with me, I'll introduce you to my stepmother."

Bright told the constables to stay in the study and followed Richard across the hall and into a large drawing room. Every possible horizontal surface in the room was covered with ornaments, silver-framed photographs and dried flower arrangements. All the people in the room seemed somehow at odds with their cluttered surroundings – all, that is, except a rather well-built lady in an old-fashioned black dress, which had probably been worn to every family funeral for the last few decades.

"Mama, this is Detective Inspector Bright. Inspector, my stepmother, Lady Ellis." Richard then turned to the two other occupants of the room. "And this is my stepsister, Margaret, and my brother, David."

Whilst the younger members of the family merely nodded and looked worried, Lady Ellis was at pains to treat Bright like any other visitor to her house.

"How do you do, Inspector? Do sit down," she said, and indicated a small Victorian button-back chair that just happened to be lower than any of the other chairs in the room.

Everybody is trying to put me at a disadvantage today, Bright thought to himself as he sat down and looked more closely at the people to whom he had just been introduced. Margaret was in her early twenties and pretty. David looked about the same age, certainly much younger than Richard, and much better looking.

It was Lady Ellis, however, who dominated the room. Over her left wrist hung an enormous and overflowing black handbag from which she periodically took a tiny white handkerchief and almost immediately returned it, snapping the clasp shut. This was her only outward sign of the strain that she must surely have been feeling.

"Now, Inspector, why do you think my husband was murdered?" she asked.

Bright cleared his throat and paused for a moment while he debated whether or not honesty would be the best policy and finally decided that it would.

"There appears to have been a large amount of air injected into his intravenous infusion. The hospital is holding an inquiry into whether or not this could have happened accidentally, but the coroner is fairly certain that it must have been deliberate."

Lady Ellis nodded her head as if this was an everyday occurrence and what she had suspected all along.

"This may seem a stupid question, but I thought it was impossible to detect if someone was killed that way?" David asked in genuine surprise.

"So did I, sir, and I am reliably informed that under certain circumstances it is undetectable. The air disperses and is dissolved in the blood. However, in this case, the murderer, if it was murder, made two mistakes.

"Firstly," Bright explained, "he committed the crime late at night and the post-mortem was naturally done first thing the next morning. Sir Edward was an important man, so they wanted to discover the cause of death quickly. In fact, they found it less than twelve hours after death." He paused to collect his thoughts and then continued. "The second mistake was in the amount of air used. Whilst the murderer had to use enough air to be certain of killing Sir Edward, he went a bit over the top and used so much that there was no chance of it all dispersing in the time available without leaving traces. Basically, the pathologist couldn't miss it."

Lecture over, Bright sat back to see what sort of effect it had had. David and Lady Ellis were looking at him with interest and Margaret was staring out of the window, but it was Richard who spoke first.

"I'm sure it is all a mistake," he said. "Some heavy-handed doctor or moronic nurse has done something wrong with an injection and is now too frightened to come forward and own up. I am sure your investigation will finally prove that it was a case of incompetence or negligence. I shall speak to Naseby when he arrives; we will have to look into the possibility of legal action of some sort."

No one looked surprised that Richard should have made up his mind to believe in the one solution which would not only remove any suspicion from the family but might also make them a bit of money.

"I don't think that's possible, Richard," David said. "Firstly, I'm pretty certain that no one could make that big a mistake. I mean, the wrong drug is one thing, but no drug at all, just a syringe full of air, isn't such an easy thing to do. Secondly, everything is double-checked, so that if one person is covering up, then another must be too. So, apart from anything else, that makes it awfully difficult to prove an error in court."

"Trust doctors to know how to protect themselves against dissatisfied customers. I suppose they have had plenty of practice at it. I dare say you will have killed a few patients by the time you retire," Richard said, only half in joke.

"Oh, I'm sure I will have; most doctors do," David agreed good-naturedly and then turned to Bright to explain. "I'm a medical student at St Bede's, in my second year of clinical work, so I only have one more year to go, and then, with a bit of luck, I will qualify. While I'm obviously not keen that this should prove to be murder, I don't personally see how it can be anything else, although I have to admit, I'm no expert."

Bright was naturally very interested in anyone who had the know-how to do the murder, especially when they were inexperienced enough to bungle it, and also admitted to having thought the method undetectable. There was also the point that, as a student at St Bede's, David would know the hospital layout and would be able to wander around at night without suspicion. He would have had no difficulty in laying his hands on a hypodermic syringe.

Bright turned his attention to Margaret, who was busy fiddling with a particularly nasty porcelain ornament of Little Boy Blue.

"What do you do for a living, Miss Ellis?" he asked and raised his eyebrows as she firmly replaced the figure and answered angrily.

"I am not Miss *Ellis*, Inspector. I am Miss Swainson. Margaret Swainson. Sir Edward was my stepfather and my mother, Lady Ellis, was his second wife."

"Thank you for putting me right, Miss Swainson. Now, perhaps you could tell me what you do for a living?"

"I am a secretary at Allan Jones & Son, in the finance department."

"Thank you. And what about you, sir?" Bright asked as he turned to Richard, who was leaning against the magnificent mantelpiece. It was a calculatedly nonchalant position which belied his extremely nervous state.

"I don't know why you are asking these questions, Inspector. They hardly seem relevant." He took a cigarette from the box by his elbow, lit it, inhaled deeply and blew smoke out through his nose as Bright answered him.

"Just making conversation whilst we wait for your solicitor, sir. I'm sorry if you don't like it. Perhaps you would like to suggest a different topic?"

"No, no, I'm sorry, Inspector," he apologised with a slight wave of his hand with its long, bony fingers. "It's just that I'm a bit on edge."

"That's quite understandable, sir, under the circumstances."

"Yes," Richard agreed thoughtfully. The fingers that held his cigarette were shaking slightly and fine beads of perspiration beaded his upper lip. "I am a stockbroker – a partner, in fact, with Johnson & Barber in the City, and I have worked there for three years."

Bright smiled at him and then looked towards the formidable Lady Ellis. She started to speak before he could even ask her a question.

"I married Sir Edward ten years ago, and it proved to be a very satisfactory arrangement for both of us. Margaret and David were at boarding school and Richard was already working and living away from home. It would not have been long before we were on our own, and neither of us wanted that. We were both too old and too sensible to require romance, and we suited each other admirably. His first wife left him fifteen years ago, and they were divorced by mutual agreement when Sir Edward and I decided to marry. He, of course, had not been knighted at that time."

She gave a slight start as the doorbell rang and tried to cover it by searching for her handkerchief. David went to answer the door and returned with a very distinguished-looking, middle-aged man who was introduced to Bright as Naseby, the family's solicitor. Bright looked enviously at Naseby's thick, dark hair with its flashes of silver at each temple and his hand went instinctively to smooth down his own receding locks.

"How do you do?" Naseby asked earnestly, holding out his hand.

"Fine, thank you. Now that you are here, Mr Naseby, perhaps we could start interviewing everyone as to where they were and what they were doing last night. I have a constable ready to take notes in the study, so it would probably be best if we used that as an office." He looked at Lady Ellis, silently asking her permission.

"Yes, that will be quite all right," she agreed.

"Do you have any servants or staff, cleaners and the like, Lady Ellis?" Bright asked.

"We have no staff who live in, but we have three who help out several days a week. One of them is here at the moment. If she's not upstairs straightening the bedrooms, she will be down in the kitchen."

"Thank you, Lady Ellis. I will just go and get myself organised and then perhaps Mr Naseby could bring you through?"

Naseby nodded and Bright went to the study.

"Johnson, there's a charlady hanging around either upstairs or in the kitchen," he said. "You go and interview her and find out about the other staff as well." As Johnson left, Bright turned to the uniformed constable. "I think it would be best if you sat over there. I want you to take brief notes as we go along. Don't worry about getting down every word at this stage. If anything interesting turns up, we'll do a formal interview and statement later."

As he finished, Naseby ushered in Lady Ellis. She sat on the chair in front of the desk and Naseby placed a chair for himself a little to one side. Bright took his place behind the desk and quickly glanced at the constable to check that he was ready.

"Right, Lady Ellis, please would you tell me everything you did between ten o'clock last night and two o'clock this morning. Try not to leave anything out; it may seem unimportant now, but it may turn out to be useful to us."

"I quite understand, Inspector, and I shall do my best." She took a deep breath and launched into her statement.

"I visited my husband in hospital earlier in the evening, leaving there at about half past eight. I drove myself back here and it was about nine o'clock when I arrived. Mary, the cook-cum-housekeeper, had left a fish pie in the oven and I did myself some frozen vegetables. I ate dinner in the kitchen and then went into the sitting room in time to see the end of the ten o'clock news on television. In fact, I came in not too long after the beginning, when they were talking about the dreadful situation in Africa. Anyway, it must have been about ten fifteen or thereabouts because after that item there was the advertisement break. When the news was over, I switched the television off and rang the hospital to find out how Edward had settled. The nurse who answered the telephone was brusque to the point of being rude. I suppose she might have been very busy, but in the old days nurses were never rude, no matter how rushed off their feet they were, but they don't seem to have the same calibre of girl now.

"After that," she continued, "I went into the kitchen and made myself some hot milk and then retired to bed with *Death of an Archangel.* Such a silly book. I guessed who did it in the first chapter. It was perfectly obvious that it was the bishop – all bishops have a certain ruthless cunning. Have to, to get where they are."

While the poor constable in the corner was frantically trying to get all this in writing, Bright was sifting through the information, trying to sort out the relevant bits, so that he might ask some intelligent questions later. To help himself more than Lady Ellis, he quickly summarised the evening's events.

"So, you were alone in the house between the salient times, but you did make a phone call at about ten forty-five to the hospital. Did anyone call you, or come to the door at all?"

"If they had, I should have told you. I was entirely on my own all evening. I went to sleep about one in the morning and slept undisturbed until eight. I got up and had a bath. Mary arrived soon after, in time to see me get my breakfast."

"Thank you, Lady Ellis, that was a very detailed account." Bright leant back in his chair and looked at her intently. "Can you tell me, Lady Ellis, did your husband have any enemies that you know about?"

"Hundreds!" she snorted. "For a start there are his own children and mine. Mind you, I don't think any of them would have the guts to murder him. There are also quite a few of his business associates who certainly will not mourn him. He knew too much about some very dubious deals and I think some people were a little frightened that he might talk about them." She waved impatiently at Naseby, who was bobbing up and down in his chair in an attempt to stop his client from saying all these things. "Do keep still, Naseby. I will say exactly what I want, so save your advice for my children. They will need it more than I."

She turned again to Bright and continued, "My husband's hands were not entirely clean, Inspector. I'm sure that you already have a good idea what I am talking about and I am quite certain that you will dig up a few rather embarrassing details about him during your investigation. He could have implicated a lot of others if he had chosen to speak up, and many of his so-called friends will sleep easier now that he is gone."

"Really, Lady Ellis, I must insist that you are more careful in what you say. It could have serious repercussions." Lady Ellis glared at Naseby, but he merely took out his cigarette case and asked, "Do you mind if I smoke?"

"I most certainly do! Kindly wait until I have left the room. I never let Edward smoke in front of me. Richard sometimes gets away with it because he is essentially a weak character and needs some sort of a prop. You don't, Naseby, so put them away."

Naseby looked at Bright and shrugged his shoulders slightly, as if to say, *She's the one who pays the bills*, and returned the cigarettes to his pocket. He seemed uncertain whether to take Lady Ellis's remark as a compliment or a criticism.

"Now, Mr Naseby, please understand that I shall say what I like. I'm not a fool and neither is the Inspector. I want to know who killed Edward and the police have more chance of finding him if they have all the facts, so I will not keep anything back which might conceivably be of help. Anyway, I thought it was against the law to withhold information."

"There is a difference between withholding information and saying so much that you complicate the issue unnecessarily."

"If you insist in continuing to interrupt this interview, Naseby, I shall ask you to leave the room," Lady Ellis stopped him. She could have been talking to an irritating schoolboy rather than to a senior partner of a distinguished law firm. Naseby flushed slightly and sat back in his seat. He knew that it was better to hear the worst than to sit outside and imagine it.

"Carry on," Lady Ellis ordered Bright.

"Thank you for being so frank, Lady Ellis. It does indeed help us. Could you perhaps give me a few more details about your husband's deals?"

"I'm afraid I don't know much about his work, Inspector, but I believe he was under investigation by the Fraud Squad, so you should be able to find out."

"Okay, I'll check that out, Lady Ellis. Now, can you possibly tell me where the first Lady, or rather Mrs Ellis, is living at present?"

"Somewhere in the south of France when we last heard. She received a very handsome settlement from Edward when they divorced, and she has been living it up ever since."

"I can give you her present address," Naseby cut in, trying a more subtle method of stopping his client.

"That is a better attitude," Lady Ellis congratulated him.

"Do you know if your husband had heard from her recently?"

"Edward certainly never mentioned it, but I am not sure that he would. There is something rather indelicate about mentioning your first wife to your second. Edward would probably feel that way about it anyway. Very silly, I suppose, but there you are. I don't think he would have told me."

"Thank you, Lady Ellis. I can't think of anything else for the moment, but perhaps I will when I know a little more about the case so I am afraid I may have to trouble you again in the future."

"Any time you like, young man; I'll give you all the information I can. No point in beating our chests and wailing. I can't stand these women who go to pieces the moment anything goes wrong. I believe Edward was murdered and I want the culprit found." She gave Bright a long, hard and determined stare, nodded to Naseby, stood up and turned to leave.

"Oh, I'm sorry, Lady Ellis, I nearly forgot one more thing." Bright smiled innocently. "I suppose it will be all right if I take a quick look through Sir Edward's papers and possessions, including the bits and pieces he had at the hospital? It won't take me long and I'll try to disturb things as little as possible."

Naseby coughed in an attempt to get Lady Ellis's attention before she answered, but she ignored him and said to Bright, "Of course. I thought you might want to do that. Look at anything you want." And she left, saying that she would send one of the others in to them.

The rest of the family were far more succinct in their statements and contented themselves with recounting their actions during the appropriate period. Margaret had been out with a boyfriend and arrived back at her flat somewhere around half past eleven. The man had stayed for coffee and left at one in the morning. Bright took the man's name and address. If he confirmed Margaret's alibi, it would effectively mean that she could not have committed the murder.

"Do you have a car?" Bright asked her.

"Yes, just a small runabout that I keep at my flat in Islington, but we used Julian's car to go to and from the restaurant."

Bright noted the name of the restaurant, Il Pescatori, and also Julian's full name and address.

David had apparently been working in his room at the medical school until about half past ten, and had then nipped down to the college bar for a quick drink. The bar had closed at eleven o'clock and David reckoned that he was back in his room about a quarter of an hour later. He had gone straight to bed, so he had no witnesses after eleven fifteen. The medical school was only five minutes' walk from the hospital, which meant that David had no alibi.

Of the three children, it was Richard who proved to be the only real headache to Naseby. He insisted on sticking to the old standby that he had been out with a lady, whom he refused to name. He said that she was married and he was anxious not to cause her any embarrassment. Naseby tried telling him he was unwise to stick to such a vague alibi, but Richard would not be moved.

"The police can be very discreet in their questioning, and if they consider it to be irrelevant, the lady's name need never come up in court," Naseby explained.

"No, no, I must at least talk to her first," Richard insisted.

"But that will devalue your alibi. I mean, if you have talked to her first, the police would have every right to suspect that you arranged it."

"That cannot be helped."

Naseby was obviously irritated by Richard's insistence but had to concede defeat.

Once they were on their own, Bright asked Naseby if he would mind answering a few questions himself.

"Not at all, Inspector, but I must warn you that I may not be at liberty to answer them all. I have my clients to consider."

"That's understood, Mr Naseby. Well, my first question is obvious. Who gets what in the last will and testament?"

Naseby cleared his throat and looked into the distance. "I would like it to be a matter of record that I did not wish to disclose the contents of the will at this stage as I have not yet spoken to the family, but felt it my duty to assist the police in their enquiries." Bright nodded and Naseby took a notepad out of his brief case and glanced at it before continuing. "Richard is heir to the main bulk of the estate. Lady Ellis is to get the residue – some odd bits of property, some money, the house here in Eaton Square, with all the furniture that is in it, bar one or two special bequests. She also keeps the Rolls-Royce and a substantial income for her lifetime, but the capital from that reverts to Richard on her demise.

"David has been left a fair number of rather dicey shares; all the better ones having been kept part of the main estate. He also has an income of five thousand pounds a year for the period that he remains at medical school and for the first five years after his qualification. Sir Edward wanted to give him the chance to set himself up in a good practice or take further qualifications as he wanted. However, if he fails his general qualification on his first attempt, he is allowed one further year in which to succeed. If he fails again at the end of that year, the allowance is stopped and everything reverts to Richard. That's a touch of good, old-fashioned bribery to work hard," he commented.

"Margaret only gets a lump sum of a couple of thousand. The three members of staff and two other employees get two or three hundred each. There are no other really substantial bequests."

Naseby looked out of the window and something about his nonchalant manner told Bright that there was a great deal more in the will. He decided to try a little gentle probing. "Just what does the bulk of the estate amount to, approximately?"

"Well, that is rather difficult to say, really. He gets Wellsworth, the country house, and farm estates in Hampshire, and enough to run it, plus a lot of paper – bonds, shares, et cetera. I suppose if he decided to turn everything into cash, he would get a couple of million, but it depends on so many things such as the stock market and so on. Richard is going to be pretty wealthy, especially since the government had a go at death duties, but a lot of the money will be tied up in running the estate. He gets the yacht as well, of course, but that isn't worth much and costs a great deal to maintain."

Bright leant back in his chair and looked at Naseby shrewdly. There had to be something he was hiding. Everything from the way he sat to the way he would not look Bright straight in the eye shouted that there was more to the will than he had said.

"Are you sure that no one else is mentioned in the will?"

Naseby thought for a moment, but he could not afford to lie to such a direct question. He flicked at a minute bit of fluff on his jacket cuff and said as casually as possible, "Miss Caroline Harris has been left a flat in St George's Square, Pimlico, and a few thousand pounds. For, um, services rendered, so to speak."

Bright whistled through his teeth and tried not to laugh. "I can see by your expression that you don't approve," he said. "Or is it just that you can see it splashed across the front of the Sunday Papers? 'Millionaire's mistress gets well paid for her services', with a juicy picture of her falling out of a natty dress and draped in mink." Bright could not stop himself from chuckling at this prospect. "What about his ex-wife? Did he remember her at all?"

"Well actually, yes, he did. He left her the villa in the south of France, and her maintenance payments are to continue to be paid out of the estate until her death."

"You mean that it wasn't her villa? This gets better and better." Bright looked as though he would have liked to rub his hands together in glee but controlled himself in time. "Sir Edward certainly wasn't playing cricket when he wrote this will. I suppose this means that he must have been on fairly friendly terms with her?"

"I really wouldn't know," Naseby said very stiffly. "Now, if that is all, I should like to go and speak to my clients."

As Naseby rose and left the room, Bright laughed to himself and set about looking through the papers in and around the desk. The top left-hand drawer revealed accounts books, bills and receipts. It would probably take the accountants weeks to sort out any discrepancies in them. Sir Edward was used to covering his tracks on the financial side of life, and from the very brief glance that Bright gave the books it did not look as though he was too straightforward even with the household and personal accounts.

"Probably covering up that he has been claiming his mistress as a housekeeping expense or something," Bright said to the constable.

He piled up all the books to be taken back to the station. None of the other drawers on the left appeared to hold anything of interest. There was only one drawer on the right and that was locked, but a quick look around the top of the desk revealed a key in the ashtray.

Inside the drawer was a loaded pistol, some more ammunition and the relevant documents. Bright unloaded the pistol and put it on top of the desk. He would have to tell Lady Ellis to lock it up properly and he would have to remind her to get the licence altered into her name, if she wished to keep it.

Having finished his search of the drawers, Bright decided to do a Sherlock Holmes bit, checking the blotting paper, but Sir Edward did not appear to use a fountain pen; the paper was quite virgin. Then he noticed that something had been slipped under it. It was a business card from a small travel agency. Bright was about to leave it when something made him slip it into his pocket before he left the room. He found Johnson in the kitchen, having a cup of coffee with the cook.

"You stay here with PC Plod in the study and do a brief search of the house," he told him. "You are looking for a syringe or anything odd. Use your initiative but don't take too long. I'll see you back at the station."

He then went to take his leave of the Ellis family and remind Lady Ellis about the pistol.

"I would also ask that no one speaks to the press at this stage. The news is bound to break sooner or later, but the longer you can put it off, the better."

"That's very good advice, Inspector. I shall speak to Mary, the housekeeper, about it as well," Lady Ellis agreed, and Naseby nodded his approval. The rest of the family seemed too caught up in their own problems to worry about the press and Bright left the house wondering if this was due solely to the understandable stress of the situation.

Chapter 3

"Okay, Hoppy, let's go over what we've got. There is enough in the way of statements and reports to sink the *QE2* but bugger all in the hard-facts line. Talk about *cherchez la femme*, we've got a whole bloody string of 'em – or rather, Sir Edward did."

Bright flicked through the notes Hoppy had made of his visit to the hospital and sat down on the desk, pushing papers and telephones out of the way with his buttock. He had loosened his tie and neatly rolled up his sleeves, ready for action of the cerebral kind.

"Now, then. Sir Edward was alive and well until eleven o'clock, or thereabouts. We have the nurses nipping in and out, with and without the doctor. Someone's lying about that drip. I see Nurse Banks says in her statement that Dr Cawthorne may have mentioned that it needed changing – she remembers him saying something but wasn't really listening at the time. I wonder if that is true, or is she just unhappy about contradicting the handsome doctor?"

"He's not exactly handsome, guv," Hoppy interjected. "In fact, I'd put him down as being wet as water."

"Don't disillusion me, Hoppy. I was under the impression that all doctors had to be Richard Chamberlain lookalikes, and in fact that it was a more important prerequisite than A levels. Please note the long word for this week: prerequisite." Bright repeated the word slowly, savouring every syllable.

"You've been reading that dictionary again and you know it's not good for you," said Hoppy. "Besides which, you've been stuck in the P section for months."

"All right, don't nag. Let's get back to the business in hand," Bright carried on. "Where were we? Oh, yes. About the eleven-thirty incident, was Nurse Jensen sure that it was Cawthorne she saw leave Sir Edward's room?"

"She seemed to be, but the light isn't very good. Whoever it was, he or she would have been silhouetted against the main corridor light, and I would have thought anyone of the same approximate build, and with a white coat, might have been mistaken for him."

"Can you draw me a rough plan of the ward and tell me which lights were on? Just so that I can visualise it better."

"Okay," said Hoppy, and he started sketching the layout of the ward. "To get to the main ward, you have to go down this little corridor branching off the main one. On either side of this little corridor are the side rooms and store rooms, bathrooms and toilets – you know the sort of thing. The main corridor light is on all night. The same goes for the sluice, or whatever they call it."

"What's that?"

"It seems to be where they put the dirty linen and clean the bedpans."

"Sounds grim. Carry on."

"There was a dim light by Sir Edward's bed so that the nurses could check his drip and so on without disturbing him, but the door is solid wood and it was left only slightly ajar, so not much light would have come from there. The reading light on the nurses' desk was also on, but that would only throw the corridor into deeper shadow. The sluice doors have small windows in them, so some light would have come from there."

"So, at eleven thirty, someone went into Sir Edward's room and it may or may not have been Dr Cawthorne?"

"Right," Hoppy agreed. "But as he opened the door to the room, some light would shine on his face."

"Not a lot, but enough perhaps?"

"It's possible, anyway," Hoppy said and then continued, "Syringes and needles are kept in the injection area here by the nurses' desk." He jabbed his pencil at the plan. "And also in the treatment room. The injection area is just a load of shelves containing the syringes, needles and a few other bits and bobs that might be needed. Obviously much more of this sort of thing is kept in the treatment room. If the murderer knew his way around, he could have gone in there and found them, but it would be difficult to get to the injection area unnoticed."

"He may have got them somewhere else completely, of course." Bright tapped the desk with a pencil and thought for a moment. "How do you think he managed to inject air into the drip without waking Sir Edward?"

"Well, he'd had that painkilling injection. What was it now?" Hoppy looked through his notebook. "Ah, yes, pethidine. Seventy-five milligrams. I suppose that would make him sleep heavier than normal, and even if he did wake up and saw someone in a white coat fiddling with his drip, he'd probably think it was nothing abnormal anyway and go back to sleep."

"That's true, provided our killer was in a white coat and Sir Edward didn't recognise him," Bright remarked.

"The light's pretty dim, only really enough for the nurses to check that the drip is still working, the patient still breathing and no blood oozing out anywhere."

"How about a bell, or call system of some kind, for if he is in distress or wants something like a bedpan?"

"There's a sort of control panel that adjusts the light, turns on the radio and calls the nurse all at once," Hoppy explained. "It's on a long cord so that it can be put next to the patient, or in his hand. It would be quite simple to move it out of reach too, and once the air had been injected it would only be a matter of seconds before Sir Edward lost consciousness and died. He may not even have woken up – at least that's what Dr Hull, the pathologist, told me," Hoppy finished on an apologetic note.

"If I didn't know that you only liked straightforward cases, Hoppy, I might think that you were getting interested in this one," Bright said with a cheeky grin. "It was ten after midnight when the body was found, wasn't it?" he asked.

"Yes, that's right. It seems the nurses do go round and check everyone as often as possible. It should be every quarter of an hour, but they were very busy that night. That tyrant of a matron or whatever read them the riot act about patients dying and no one knowing for certain when it had happened."

"No, well, it doesn't look good. Besides which, if I were in hospital and had a quiet heart attack, I'd like someone to try and get me going again fairly soon after it, not an hour or so later when rigor mortis has set in. Right, so Sir Edward pegged it somewhere between ten forty-five and twelve ten, which fits in with the pathologist's estimate. Did any of the doctors or nurses on the scene have anything more to say about that?"

"The anaesthetist in charge of the crash team that tried to revive Sir Edward said that the body was just beginning to cool down when they arrived, which he said puts the time of death at less than three-quarters of an hour beforehand but probably more than a quarter of an hour – say between eleven thirty and midnight, as it took them a few minutes to arrive."

"So, we have a strange person in a white coat, possibly Dr Cawthorne, entering the room at eleven thirty, and Sir Edward may have died then or soon after. It's looking more and more like murder to me, Hoppy. I've requested that the inquest be delayed as long as possible. Even if they only take evidence on cause of death and not responsibility, the press'll start getting suspicious. Mind you, if we delay it too long, they'll smell a rat anyway." Bright paused for a moment. "Any other interesting snippets of information come to light at St B's?"

"Well, I don't know how much importance to attach to it, but I overheard the dean say to the consultant that no mention should be made of Cawthorne's past record, so maybe we should have a little nose around there."

"I'd say it might be interesting, yes. We also want to find out if any of the staff involved are matey with young David Ellis." Bright stood up and felt in his trouser pocket for a handkerchief and cleaned his glasses before continuing, "Pity about not finding any out-of-place fingerprints anywhere. I had hoped for just one on the buzzer or bedhead, but they obviously clean too well at St B's, or perhaps the killer wore gloves. There must be no end of surgical gloves in a hospital. It's the sort of place that is designed especially to help the would-be murderer and hinder the poor policeman. I bet Denison made himself unpopular taking prints from all the patients."

Hoppy chuckled. "I think they found it rather exciting, but I did hear that he nearly got assaulted by a pint-sized Filipino cleaner who thought he was checking for illegal immigrants!"

"Poor Denison, so misunderstood. How about Sir Edward's personal effects?" Bright asked, returning to the point. "Anything interesting there?"

"Not really. They're all downstairs if you want to inspect them. There was a girlie magazine that he probably bought off the hospital trolley – they're really getting with it, aren't they, although I wouldn't have thought that he was feeling up to it myself. Perhaps one of his sons brought it in for him. Oh, and there was a card that had obviously come with some flowers and was in his wallet. It was typed and said:

> Prolonging my stay here.
> Don't hang around in hospital.
> Caroline.

"I only mention it because it's not the most normal thing to say on a get-well card."

"No, but hardly suspicious, is it?"

"No. Oh, and there was a flask of whisky too – I doubt if the matron would be pleased to know he'd got that; I mean he wasn't supposed to be having anything by mouth."

"I don't know though, Hoppy. After all, it does kill off the bugs," Bright said with a slight smile. He stood up and stretched tiredly. "Dingwall's requested a report on Sir Edward and his dealings from the City Fraud Squad. They've promised we'll have it later tomorrow." He looked at his watch. "Bloody hell! Only five minutes before the evening briefing. I'll have to get a move on. So, you reckon at least another day and a half before all the initial actions at the hospital are finished?"

Hoppy nodded.

"And I'm going to need two more people to help check alibis." Bright thought for a moment, pulling at the hairs of his neat ginger beard. "I've got to have more people on overtime, so I had better go along and plead with the super. I'll be back in a tick. Hold the fort for me," he said, and almost ran along the corridor to the chief superintendent's office.

* * *

"Right, lads, you're all up to date with what's going on now, so here's the bad news. I need six constables to go back to the hospital. We've got to interview all the night staff – everyone: porters, cleaners, doctors and nurses. Everyone. Someone must have seen our murderer wandering about the place. Sergeant Hopwood will be going with you."

He looked around for volunteers but there were only four, so he volunteered a couple more.

"Dingwall, you could probably do with a bit of fresh air, so you and I will go alibi-checking. I'll see the rest of you back here at eight o'clock sharp for the morning briefing, and you had better all be prepared to work at least a twelve-hour day; we want quick results on this one." He picked up his jacket and left the room. As he walked down the corridor, he could hear the chorus of moans from the majority and the occasional cheer from someone who was particularly short of money.

* * *

Julian Penfold was in when Bright and Dingwall knocked at the door of his flat, but he was not alone.

"Do come on in, Inspector," he said, with an extravagantly clumsy gesture of his long arms. "As you can see, Margaret is here. We, um, didn't expect you to come round tonight. Not that it matters, of course." He gave an anxious smile.

"Good evening, Miss Swainson. I'm sorry to disturb you again."

"Not at all, Inspector, I was just leaving. I'll see you tomorrow, will I, Julian?" she asked as she stood up.

"I'll come round after work, Margaret. I'll try to make it early if possible." Julian closed the sitting room door as he showed Margaret out. Bright moved closer to it and strained his ears, but was unable to hear their muttered conversation. As the front door closed, he moved away again and was busy examining a carriage clock on the mantelpiece when Julian returned.

"Sorry about that, Inspector. Do sit down both of you. Can I get you a drink?"

"No, thank you very much, sir. This is just a routine matter. It shouldn't take long. Could you just tell us what you were doing last night?"

"Well yes, I was with Margaret," he replied and folded his long, thin body into an armchair and stretched his legs out in front of him. "We went out to dinner, at an Italian place in Highbury, and then we went back to Margaret's place for coffee. I stayed for a while and then I came back here."

"And do you perhaps know the approximate times that you did all of these things?"

"Well, I believe it was around eleven when we left the restaurant, and one or so when I left Margaret."

"You couldn't be a little more precise about that, could you, sir?"

"Well, no, actually, Inspector," Julian explained with some embarrassment. "You see, I'd had rather a lot to drink and don't actually remember much about the evening. To be honest with you, I was pissed as a newt and that's why Margaret threw me out. I walked back here and passed out. I was in a dreadful state this morning: diabolical hangover, late for work and I had to walk all the way over to Margaret's to pick up my car – after I remembered where I had left it, that is."

"I see, sir. So what made you think that you left Margaret's at one o'clock?"

"Well, I don't really know, to be honest. It just seems to be right, that's all. I know I was there for quite a while."

"Miss Swainson didn't mention it at all, then?"

"No. Well, I mean not deliberately. She did just happen to mention it, but I'm sure she's right, and honestly, Inspector, I know it looks bad but she wouldn't lie about it."

"No, sir. Of course not. I don't suppose there is anyone else who can confirm any of this, is there?"

"No, I'm afraid not. I'm not much use, am I, Inspector?" Julian asked candidly.

"Not a lot, to be honest, sir, but it gives us something to work on at least. These things happen to the best of us; it's just rather a shame you picked last night!"

"Believe me, Inspector, I've been regretting it all day."

* * *

The next stop was Il Pescatori, the restaurant used by Julian and Margaret the night before. It was a small and extremely aromatic bistro, romantically candle-lit. A waiter approached them and tried to show them to a table.

"No, no, we don't want to eat," Bright explained. "I am a police officer. Look, here's my warrant card. I want to speak to the staff who were working here last night."

The waiter looked at Bright's proffered card and then went to the back of the restaurant and spoke to another man. A third man was called over and the three of them talked and gesticulated and frequently glanced at Bright and Dingwall. The oldest among them finally shrugged and came over, ignoring a customer who was desperately trying to catch his eye.

"What is this, Inspector?" he asked in heavily accented English. "What is this all about?"

"We want some information about two people who had dinner here last night: a lady in her early twenties, slim, short, dark hair and five foot two or three, and a man a little older, light-brown hair cut short, and about six foot two or so. Does anyone remember them at all?"

The other two waiters were called forward and there was a long discussion in Italian, finishing with a series of nods all round.

Again it was the older man who spoke.

"Last night, we had one large party and three couples only. It is a quiet night, you see. We remember a couple that were like you say, we think. The lady, she comes here often. The table had been booked, so I can check the book for you, yes?"

"That would be great, yes."

He picked up the diary on the desk by the door and turned to the page of the night before.

"The table was booked by a Mr Penfold, for nine o'clock."

"Good, that's the right couple. Now, can you tell me what time they left?"

"It was about a quarter to eleven, maybe a little later, when they left. I know because I helped them to their car myself. They were only parked a little way down the road."

The customer who had been trying to attract someone's attention called to them in exasperation and the youngest of the waiters reluctantly went to serve him.

"Do you often help customers out?" Bright asked.

"No sir, but Mr Penfold had drunk a little too much, I think. So you see, I thought it best to help him to his car."

"I do see, indeed; but was he fit to drive home, then?"

"Oh no, he did not drive. He couldn't even stand. It was the lady who drove away."

"And this was at about a quarter to eleven?"

"Yes, maybe a little later, but certainly before eleven o'clock."

"Thank you, you've been a great help."

As they walked back to the car, Bright seemed thoughtful.

"We'll have to do a house-to-house around the two flats – Swainson's and Penfold's. I'll send some people tomorrow morning, but they both live in the sort of area where ninety per cent of the residents will be out at work, so we'll probably have to send another team in the evening. Still, if he was so drunk that Margaret threw him out, he could well have been a bit noisy. You never know, he might have sung rugger songs at the top of his voice or knocked over a dustbin or something. Mind you, even if he did, nobody will have heard."

* * *

It was about half past nine the following morning when Bright knocked at the door of room 120 in the nurses' home attached to St Bede's. The door was quickly opened and a very pale and worried face looked out.

"I'm sorry to disturb you, but I was hoping to catch you before you went to bed. My name's Detective Inspector Bright and I'd just like to ask you a couple of questions. It won't take very long."

The girl ran a hand through her untidy, mouse-coloured hair and opened the door a fraction further to reveal a severely sensible dressing gown.

"Of course, do come in. I'm afraid this has all got me down and I'm always a bit groggy when I'm on night duty anyway."

She opened the door wide and Bright went into the tiny box-like room, with a built-in cupboard and a small bed neatly fitted under the bookshelf. It was all very shabby and utilitarian and the few posters and ornaments that should have made it more homely somehow only made it more pathetic.

"I didn't realise they still kept you in these places. I thought most of the hospitals had built modern blocks of flats for the staff."

"The new blocks are only for qualified staff at St Bede's," Nurse Banks replied with a grimace, and then added, "Mind you, I'm one of the lucky ones. A lot of my friends still live in the Central. You know, the old loony bin. It's not really fit for human habitation, but as the nurses have nowhere else to go, they're still there, for the time being anyway."

She hastily removed her uniform from the only chair in the room and motioned to Bright to sit down on it while she perched on the end of the bed.

"How did you get past the dragon in reception? We aren't allowed visitors in our rooms at this hour of the morning."

"Oh, I just flashed my card and told her I was on official business. I don't think she believed me, but not many people argue with a policeman."

She smiled tentatively and Bright realised that under different circumstances she could be a happy and pretty young girl instead of the rather sad and dismal sight that she had at first seemed.

"I just wanted to ask you if you could tell me, in your own words, exactly what happened. Oh, I know you've told us everything already," he said forestalling her, "but I want to get the feel of how it was."

She reluctantly agreed and, as she told her story, the last vestiges of her nervousness disappeared and were replaced by deep furrows of concentration as she tried to give him a detailed and accurate account of the events. It was the same as she had said before, except over one important point.

"And just as Dr Cawthorne was leaving, he said something about the bag being empty. So you see Nurse Jensen must have made a mistake about putting it up before going to the loo. She's very frightened by all this and I think she's worried that any blame might be put on her. She wants so desperately to do well. On night duty you tend to get to know people quicker than you would normally, and tell them things about yourself that maybe you wouldn't in other circumstances. Shirley – Nurse Jensen, I mean – told me that she hasn't done awfully well in her first-year exams and has been given a warning that if her ward reports are not up to standard then she'll be asked to leave. I'm sure she's just trying to cover herself and I can't say that I blame her." She would not look Bright in the eye but stared alternately at her fingers and out of the window. Two red spots burned brightly on her cheeks.

"You know it's not a good idea to bend the truth, love," Bright said gently. "I know what you've just said is basically what you said before, only a little more favourable to Dr Cawthorne, but it's not exactly the truth, is it? You won't help anyone with all this covering up and you certainly won't help yourself. Now, maybe you're right and Nurse Jensen is lying to make sure she stays clean, but it's not up to you to put a spoke in her wheel by lying too." He gave her a pat on the knee and a sympathetic look, but to his dismay she sniffed loudly and reached for a tissue.

"I don't know what to do. I should never have lied, but he told me I had to, and I'd do anything to help him. He told me, if I didn't, he'd be for the high jump because of what happened before." She stopped to catch her breath and wipe away a tear. "When I'd done it, I wanted to come and tell your sergeant, whatever his name is, but he said I'd be in trouble and lose my job because I'd committed perjury. I've been so frightened and I didn't know what to do. I just can't seem to think clearly at the moment." She sobbed, sniffed, wiped her nose on the back of her hand and belatedly remembered her tissue. *And I thought they taught these nurses hygiene*, Bright said to himself.

"Now don't you worry about a thing," he told her. "You haven't committed perjury yet, but if you had carried on and given false information at the inquest, that would have been different. So, am I right in guessing that 'he' is Dr Cawthorne?"

Nurse Banks nodded miserably and sniffed again.

"And you didn't see him come back later?"

"No. No, I told the truth about that, honestly."

"Okay, don't worry about that. You mentioned that something had happened to Dr Cawthorne before. Can you tell me about that?"

"I really don't think I ought to, Inspector. I really shouldn't have mentioned it at all. It has absolutely nothing to do with this and you'll get the wrong idea about Dr Cawthorne."

"Now don't you go telling me what I should or shouldn't know about anyone concerned with this case," he scolded. "You must remember that I'm the one who decides what is or isn't relevant, but I can't do that until I know the facts. Besides, if you don't tell me, you will be withholding information, and that's wrong. Now, what did Dr Cawthorne do that's so dreadful?"

She hesitated for a moment before explaining.

"About a year ago, he made a mistake with a dosage and gave some old lady ten times the amount of an IV drug that he should have done and she died. I don't know all the circumstances, but I'm sure it was just a stupid mistake. You should have asked Charles to tell you – you see how bad it looks, but really there is no connection between the two cases. It's just a dreadful coincidence that he was Sir Edward's doctor too. It's not the same at all to give the wrong dose of a drug as to inject air. The hospital hushed it all up, about the old lady I mean, but he's still on trial really, you see. Another mistake and he'll be out on his ear. She was an old lady and dying anyway and it was probably a relief, both for her and her relatives. I know it's wrong to say that, but it was only a small mistake, and it killed her, that's what's so unfair. Even a small mistake, made by a doctor or nurse, can have dreadful consequences and ruin their careers. Nobody understands that we are only human."

"Don't worry, love, I'll be discreet. As you say, it's probably got nothing to do with this case, but it's just as well I know because it saves me being suspicious about it. Now, just one more question and then I'll let you be. Did Lady Ellis phone that night, and if so, what time was it?"

"Oh gosh, I can't really remember. Yes, she did ring. That's right, I certainly remember that. Now, what time was it?" She stopped and stared intently at the ceiling, happier again now they were on safer ground.

"I was just checking the new drip with Shirley Jensen, who was saying that she wanted to go to the loo. Mr Childs was calling out and the prostatectomy's bladder washout had just run through, so I think I was a bit rude to her on the phone. I just didn't have time to talk. She's such an intimidating woman, just like the PNO. I always do the wrong thing in front of someone like that."

Bright knew exactly what she meant. "So, would you say that she rang about ten forty-five?"

"Yes, somewhere around then. I'm sorry I can't be more exact."

"That's okay. Right, you know the empty ward where they are doing all the interviews?"

She nodded.

"You'd better nip down there sometime today and tell them everything you've told me. We'll take it down as a formal statement because we may have to use it as evidence at the inquest."

"Does that mean that they won't need me there to give evidence?"

"I don't know yet, but you can live in hope. Anyway, I'll let Sergeant Hopwood know that you'll be coming to make a statement. Thanks for all your help. I'll be off now and leave you to your sleep."

She seemed relieved that he was going and quickly closed the door behind him.

* * *

Bright was whistling as he left Anderson Ward, where six uniformed constables, under the eagle eye of Sergeant Hopwood, were busy conducting interviews. Four more constables were interviewing patients in the wards. He stopped a young nurse to ask the way to the medical college and she pointed to a narrow passage between two buildings.

"It's through there, if you can get by all the rubbish. You turn right at the end and a couple of hundred yards along you'll see the gates."

Bright went down the passage to what appeared to be the tradesmen's entrance to the hospital. There were piles of large black plastic bags, all full and overflowing with rubbish. As he picked his way past them, Bright saw a man, dressed in a pair of dirty blue overalls, leaning against the wall and watching Bright intently.

"Amazing, innit, how much rubbish one 'ospital can make in a couple of days?"

They both looked again at the bags.

"Bet yer ain't never seen so much rubbish in your life."

"No, I haven't," Bright agreed. "I would've thought that it would be a health hazard, leaving it there like that. Don't they burn it every day?"

"Normally they do, see? But the porters won't do it 'cos they're a load of wet bastards and it ain't my job to load the incinerator, so I won't do it neither."

He was about to wander off when Bright stopped him.

"So, none of the rubbish from anywhere in the hospital has been burnt for the last two days?"

"Well, they was burning it, first thing yesterday morning when they called the strike. They'd only just started, see? So that was the day before's rubbish they was doing and none's been done since. Still, they'll get it sorted soon and then they'll get plenty of overtime pay to burn what should've been burnt before."

Bright nodded in agreement and wandered off, deep in thought.

* * *

Once he reached the medical school, it did not take him long to find the porter's desk. It was manned most days by a small, middle-aged man with the unlikely name of Bruno. His job was to deal with telephone calls, sort mail and watch the students come and go. He seemed to know more about the students than their own mothers and certainly more than the students would have liked their mothers to know!

While Bruno often worked odd extra shifts and overtime, the desk was never manned after nine o'clock at night. The students then had to answer the telephones themselves. As Bruno had left for home at half past eight on the night of the murder, he did not know whether or not David Ellis had been in the bar or for how long.

"However," he added, "if young David said he left the bar a quarter of an hour after it had closed, it was more likely to be three fifteen than eleven fifteen. He's probably trying to protect the bar staff, seeing as you are a policeman, but you see the bar doesn't really keep to its proper hours. Provided everybody behaves himself and there is no trouble, then the authorities let them be. In fact, the bar tends to close when the barman wants to go to bed, or when all the customers pass out."

Bruno laughed, but at the same time he was watching Bright anxiously for signs of disapproval.

"If you want to know who was behind the bar that night, I suggest you go and talk to the president of the wine committee, who keeps a list of who is on duty and when. Whoever was behind the bar might remember some of his customers and they in turn might be able to tell you when David was in the bar, but I wouldn't bank on it if I were you."

"Thanks, that sounds like a good idea. Perhaps you could help me to find him, as well?"

The president of the wine committee proved to be a relatively easy man to find; he was still in bed, obviously having had a heavy drinking session the night before. He was not too pleased at being disturbed and it took him a few minutes to locate the list of bar staff, finally finding it under a pile of girlie magazines.

The list showed that two people had run the bar that night, Samuel Ingoldsby and Fiona Warfield, and Bruno successfully located them both. Fiona was, surprisingly enough, in a lecture, but Samuel was in the reading room, looking at the *Daily Star* and waiting for the pubs to open. He was a huge great bear of a prop forward in the first XV.

"I can't exactly remember when David left," he confided amiably. "I'd had a few by then and it's all rather hazy. David was definitely in the bar though, because there was a bit of a rumpus over some girl or other. I seem to remember she was quite pretty and was a bit upset over it all. I don't know who she was though. I'm sorry I'm not being much help, but I'm sure you understand." He grinned at Bright, revealing several gaps in his teeth.

"Do you remember any of the other people who were in the bar that night? I may be able to get more specific information from them."

As Sam quickly reeled off a list of names, Bright struggled to write them all down. It seemed that most of the hospital staff had been in the bar at some stage. Rather than try to track them all down, Bright asked Bruno to stick up a notice, asking everyone who was in the bar that night to be in the reading room at five o'clock.

* * *

Leaving the medical school, he decided to return to the hospital as it was too early to take Hoppy off to lunch. Dr Cawthorne was busy in theatre and could not be disturbed, so he wandered along to the "scene" of the crime.

Hailey Ward was old-fashioned in its design, and all the beds were visible from the nurses' desk, except for those in the two side rooms. The injection area, where all such treatments were prepared, was directly in front of the desk. A member of the medical staff would have no problem taking a syringe and needle, but it would be virtually impossible for a member of the public to do so undetected. That only left the treatment room, just off the entry corridor, but the door to that was kept closed, if not locked, and few people would have known where to find it.

At the end of the corridor was a pile of the now familiar black rubbish bags, and Bright asked the ward sister exactly what the strike was all about.

"Well, it's all to do with the disposal of sharps – dirty needles, broken glass and the like," she explained. "You see, the nurses are supposed to put everything like that into these special rigid containers, which are then loaded straight into the incinerator by the porters. However, occasionally a stray needle gets into the ordinary rubbish bags and an unsuspecting porter may get jabbed by it when shifting the bags. I believe that is exactly what happened yesterday. Anyway, the porters are making their feelings known and also asking for special protective gloves. I think they have a good point because it's not just the cut or whatever, but quite often the needles are infected and there is a strong chance of catching hepatitis or even AIDS. The injured porter has to have painful antibody injections and a medical follow-up and often worries over what was really a very minor injury. I can't understand why they haven't been given gloves before as a simple and reasonable precaution. The administrators are making a big song and dance about it as usual but they'll have to give way in the end. It won't cost them much but their pride."

Bright admired both her common sense and her intolerance of those in authority who lacked it, but he had not time to stay and talk; he had to see the administrators before they settled the dispute. He wanted the mountain of rubbish!

Chapter 4

Bright met Hoppy for lunch in the back bar of the Anglesey, and the two of them discussed the case over a meal of pie and chips washed down with bitter.

"What do you reckon are the odds on Richard, eh Hoppy?" Bright asked.

"Personally, I'd put my money on the medical one, guv. Of course I haven't met the happy family yet, and I gather Richard isn't what you'd call charming, but I bet if you did a bit of digging near any of them, you'd find a few skeletons refusing to stay locked up in their cupboards. By the way." Hoppy paused to catch a wayward chip and replace it in his mouth. "Coroner wants the inquest the day after tomorrow."

"Hell! That doesn't give us much time. Just because the corpse is some sort of a VIP, they want to rush him into a grave with indecent haste." Bright took a long pull of beer and set his glass down on the soggy mat. "We are going to have to ask for a team to sort through all that hospital rubbish. God only knows what we'll find. Well, I can probably hazard a guess, as it happens: a lot of grimy dressings, filthy disposable medical equipment and things beyond even my sordid imagination. I doubt that we'll find anything of value, but forensics are going to love checking everything for fingerprints, just in case. I've got this nagging feeling that we might just turn up something of interest – you know, like a doctor's disguise kit or several thousand possible murder weapons. It will take time, though, and I'll have to see if the super will give me a few extra constables, but he's not going to like it and the hospital won't think much of it either. If having the rubbish lying there in its bags is a health hazard, it will be much worse when we tip it all out on the ground."

"Couldn't we remove it and do the sifting elsewhere?"

"That's a thought, but there's just so much of the wretched stuff, I don't really think it's feasible. What we'll have to do is to have some men sifting and others putting the sifted rubbish straight back into bags. I'll try and arrange it for tomorrow but it's a bloody scumbag of a job for the poor sods."

"You aren't exactly going to be popular with the lads."

"That's the way it goes, I'm afraid, Hoppy. Us leaders are destined to be hated by our men, but do we let it get us down? No, we do our duty and make sure they do the dirty work." With a grin, Bright got up and pushed his way to the bar, leaving Hoppy to clean, scrape and finally refill his pipe. When he came back, he was muttering to himself.

"Perspicacity, Perspicacity," he repeated, rolling the word around his tongue. "Perspic–"

"I wish you'd move on from the P's," Hoppy interrupted rudely. "In fact, I wish you'd hurry up and finish the whole ruddy dictionary. I can't think why you want to go learning all these long words anyway."

"I want to get promoted, Hoppy, and if I can talk proper, I mean properly, it can only help."

"You're far more likely to get promotion if you find out who killed Sir Edward Ellis than if you go around using great long words that nobody understands anyway."

"You think I'm a pedant, Hoppy," Bright continued cheerfully. "A pedant – that's what you think I am."

"Your personal quirks are best kept between you and your girlfriends. They are nothing to do with me." Hoppy got up in disgust. "Well, even if you haven't got any work to do, I have, so I'll see you at the evening briefing."

"I'd best be off too, Hoppy. I'll go back and arrange that rubbish sifting and find out what's been happening. Oh, and I'll be back here, or rather at the medical school, at five, so could you send two of your lot across to help interview the medical students who were in the bar? If they see the college porter, Bruno, he'll show them where to go!"

"Right," Hoppy said, and they both left the overcrowded pub.

Back at the station, Bright met Dingwall, who had spent the morning checking alibis. He had discovered that Mrs Ellis the first had been in London on a shopping trip and in fact was still staying at a small hotel in South Kensington. Miss Caroline Harris, however, was well out of the way, on holiday in America. While checks would have to be done to make sure that she had not slipped back into Britain just long enough to kill Sir Edward, it did not seem very likely, and Bright felt that to all intents and purposes they could eliminate her from the suspect list.

"Let's pop over and see Mrs Ellis number one before I have to go back to the medical college and talk to the students," he said.

Just as they were leaving, a policewoman came in to the incident room. "There's a lady to see you, sir," she said.

"Oh yes? Who is she then?"

"Wouldn't give her name, sir. She just said that it was urgent and confidential."

"Okay. Well, take her along to the interview room, will you? I'll see the lady straight away."

"Do you want me to come along as well, guv?" Dingwall asked.

"Indeed I do, Dingwall. I bet you a fiver this turns out to be Richard's married lady."

She was already seated in the spartanly furnished interview room when they arrived, but she half-turned towards them and simpered, "Inspector Bright, I presume?"

"Don't tell me, your name's Stanley."

"No, no, it isn't," she said in a puzzled voice.

"No, I don't suppose it is. So, what did you want to see me about then, madam?"

She touched her dark, shoulder-length hair. It was so rigidly held in place with hair spray that it did not move. "Well, I'd rather like a word with you on your own, Inspector. If you know what I mean?"

"This is DC Dingwall, madam, and he is discretion personified. He is also staying here, so shall we begin?"

Bright's uncompromising response disconcerted her. She seemed uncomfortable in her ultra-respectable and conservative clothes, which were at variance not just with her over made-up face but also with the large amounts of flashy jewellery she was wearing. She had rings on all her fingers, including a wide and ornate gold wedding band and an engagement ring set with a huge amethyst. She fiddled with these rings as she tried again.

"Well, it's all rather difficult," she said, still trying to look dumb and appealing, but only succeeding in looking the former.

"Perhaps I can help you then," Bright cut in. "You want to tell me about a boyfriend of yours, who stayed the night and now needs an alibi. However, you are concerned that your husband should not find out about all this."

"How on earth did you know? I mean, about Richard and me."

"It wasn't so very difficult. We were wondering when you would come forward. Now, I think perhaps we had better start with your name and address."

"I'm sure you don't really need my name, Inspector. I mean, Richard was with me the whole time, so he couldn't have killed his father. It's impossible for him to have done it, so why do you need my name?"

"For the record."

"Well, what if I were to give you a false name?"

"Then the alibi you give Richard is worthless."

"But I'm not too happy about all this. Can I just have your word that my husband will never hear about any of this?"

"My word means nothing, so you can certainly have it, but I must tell you that if the coroner requires it or if it is necessary in a court of law, you will have to testify for Richard and support his alibi. If you refuse to do this, you can be subpoenaed anyway. So I strongly advise you to tell us the whole truth now and trust to luck and Richard that he is completely out of the running."

She twisted the grotesque rings round and round on her fingers while she thought. Bright did not believe for one moment that her husband gave a damn who she slept with, always supposing he was still around to know, but it was too early for her to give up the pretence yet.

"All right," she finally agreed and added melodramatically, "For Richard, I will tell you everything. My husband has to spend a lot of time away from home owing to the nature of his work," she explained.

"And what exactly is the nature of your husband's work?"

"I'm sure you don't really need to know all these personal details, Inspector. It is surely enough for you to know that last Monday night Richard Ellis was with me from eight in the evening until about four o'clock the next morning, and if necessary, I am prepared to go to court and testify to that effect. There are no other witnesses because we stayed in all night."

"Okay, we'll play it your way. Let us just have your name and address before you dash off. It would be a terrible shame if, after all the trouble you've been to,

Richard was once more left without an alibi because we had no means of contacting you."

Despite these words, he actually gave the impression that there was nothing he would like more. She reluctantly gave them her name and address, but Bright, having gained the initiative, decided to ask for more.

"DC Dingwall here will just take your fingerprints as well, if you don't mind. Purely routine, I assure you. Doesn't take a minute and hardly makes a mess at all." While she almost certainly would have liked to refuse, Bright had not given her the chance.

When Dingwall returned from the fingerprinting, Bright was still sitting at the interview-room table. The fluorescent light was flickering, highlighting how little natural light filtered through the heavily reinforced glass of the windows.

"Let's get her checked out as quickly as possible," he said, glancing at the notepad. "Desiree de Loro. God, what a name!" and they went back upstairs.

"I'll do it now, guv, but I bet she's clean, just short of money and low on morals."

"Everyone who is short of money is low on morals, if they've any sense." Bright commented cynically as Dingwall typed the information into the incident-room terminal.

"Come on, Dingwall, let's leave the computer to do its bit. Sergeant Harper will check the results. What were we about to do before we were so rudely interrupted? Oh yes, visit the ex-Mrs Ellis. What time is it?" He looked at his watch. "Four thirty. I'm sure I had something else on this afternoon." He tapped his teeth with his index finger and stared at the ceiling thoughtfully. "Oh, hell! I asked all those students to meet at five o'clock at the medical college. Come along, we'll have to rush if we're going to get there."

It was the wrong time of day to be travelling in the City of London. The nine-to-five day has long been a myth and it was obvious from the traffic jams that most of the office workers had set off for home at about four o'clock.

"It's a conspiracy. They're having a competition to see just how stupid they can be and someone forgot to let me know." Bright tried to change lanes, but someone cut in front of him and blocked the way. "Can you believe it? He didn't even bother to signal, the pillock." He thumped the steering wheel in frustration.

They edged slowly along in silence for a while before Bright asked, "What exactly do they suspect in that corruption business? It was something about taking bribes and fiddling who got various council and government contracts, wasn't it?"

"I don't really know much about it, guv, but I think that was the rough idea. Construction jobs of some kind I think, anyway. Probably motorways, tower blocks and the like."

They turned into the square and slid through the medical school gates.

"I wonder if there is a connection with Richard?" Bright murmured quietly as they came to a halt alongside a no-parking sign. "I wonder."

Chapter 5

As Bruno showed them into the reading room, Bright saw to his relief that the two policemen sent to help had not waited and were already interviewing the first students. Four small rooms, normally used for quiet study, had been prepared for them, each with a table and two chairs. A restless mob was waiting outside, sitting in chairs and on the floor and vociferously complaining about the waste of their time.

Bright cleared his throat to get their attention.

"If you could listen for one moment, please." The noise gradually stopped and everyone turned to look at who was talking. "We are here because of certain crimes that occurred in the hospital the night before last. We want to build up a complete picture of the night's events and to help give us the background we need to know what happened in the bar. All we want is for you to say at what times you were in the bar, who you saw, or talked to, and if anything unusual happened."

He turned to go into his interview room, but stopped and caught Bruno's eye and called him over.

"I'd like to see the other person that was behind the bar first of all. I think her name was Fiona Warfield. Perhaps you could point her out or send her in."

"Certainly, sir. I know she's in here somewhere, I'll just go and find her for you."

Bright went into his room and sat down behind the table. He took out his notebook and a well-chewed ballpoint pen and scribbled on the paper to see if it worked. He looked up as the door opened and a friendly face peered round.

"Come in, Miss Warfield," he said, wishing that there was a stool around for him to stand on and quickly gesturing for her to sit down. It always irritated him when a woman was considerably taller than himself. He knew that it was stupid and a sign of his insecurity, but it was something that he could not help, and Fiona Warfield certainly was a big lass. As well as being nearly six feet tall, she did not have an exactly sylph-like figure either. Apart from the biggest boobs Bright had seen for a long while, it looked as though she was all muscle. Her chest was encased in a very tight T-shirt emblazoned with the motto "Big is better", and in that particular area, Bright agreed with her.

* * *

Once she was settled in her chair, he asked her to tell him everything she remembered from the time the bar had opened that Monday night. If she were anything like Sam that would not be much, he thought.

"Well, we opened the bar at ten, ready for the people coming out from the film show. Every Monday night the film club meet to see something either pornographic or excessively violent, and they are usually out and dying of thirst by ten thirty. When we went to open up there were a couple of people already waiting."

She played with her straight blondish hair, which she wore loose, while she told Bright their names and he dutifully noted them down. She carried on telling him who came in and when, to the best of her ability, and that seemed to be better than the average witness. At least her memory had not been blurred by over-indulgence.

"I believe you are really interested in David Ellis and I remember him coming in sometime after we had opened but before the crowds arrived from the film club, so it must have been between ten twenty and half past. He came up to the bar and asked me for a pint of bitter and a gin and tonic."

Bright looked up quickly and asked, "Who was the gin and tonic bought for?"

"Indeed, for whom was the gin and tonic bought?" she corrected lightly.

Bright gave her a very cold look and she immediately apologised.

"I'm very sorry, that was incredibly rude of me. I do hope you will forgive me." Her rather plain face lit up as she smiled.

"Now, where were we?" she continued. "Oh yes, there wasn't anybody actually with him, but I assumed that he had arranged to meet someone after the film and was getting in the drinks before the crowds arrived."

"That seems a pretty logical explanation. Can you remember if it is what actually happened?"

"Well, everyone came in at once then, and it all became a bit hectic. I can't remember seeing him until quite a time later."

"Can you tell me everyone that you remember coming in at that time, just so we can ask them if anyone did meet him?"

She began to give him a few names, but seemed more uncertain than before, and she suddenly blurted out, "David wouldn't do anything wrong, you know. I thought we were just asked here to confirm his alibi, but as you didn't know that he had met anyone in the bar, I'm a bit worried. Oh, I know it's my duty to tell you everything and all that rot, but I would feel terrible if I dropped someone right in it or something," she finished lamely.

"I quite understand; it's never nice to shop a friend. But let me reassure you, David has not given us any kind of an alibi. He told us that he was on his own in the bar and then went to bed at eleven fifteen, again on his own, but I am beginning to suspect that, for some reason, he is not telling the truth. So, you see, anything that you tell me has got to be an improvement. He has put himself in an awkward position in order to hide something that probably has nothing to do with the case anyway."

"Oh, I see. That's all right then, I think," she said dubiously and then continued with more certainty, "I remember David coming back to the bar quite a long time later. I didn't serve him. Sam did, or it might have been Joe. We were so busy by that time, you see, that I had roped Joe in to help us."

"Sam didn't mention that," Bright said with a smile. "Mind you, he didn't remember much about the evening at all!"

"Sam never does," she laughed. "I'm sure he drinks more than he serves. That's why I was so relieved when Joe offered to help. We were really quite busy and there is nothing worse than a half-drunk medic being kept waiting for his next drink. They have this nasty tendency to get a bit aggressive."

"From the brief glimpse I got of the crowd next door, I can well believe it."

"Anyway, about eleven o'clock, a vile toad by the name of Jeremy Pratt, and believe me it's apt, came up to the bar and asked me if I had seen David around. I said that he certainly had been earlier on but I couldn't be certain whether or not he had left. Someone, whose name I don't know but I think he's a second year, said that David was in a dark corner with a pretty nurse, and then smirked. Jeremy didn't seem very happy at this. I believe he has been forcing his attentions on a first-year student nurse recently. She was obviously too polite in her refusals and has subsequently had to spend her time avoiding him.

There's no point in being subtle or polite with berks like Jeremy; they never understand what you mean. Anyway, Jeremy disappeared off into the back room, looking for David."

"And did he find him?" Bright was getting so carried away listening to the story that he had forgotten to take any notes for the past few minutes.

"Well, you can't see the room at the back from the bar and with all the people and noise I couldn't hear anything, but I was told later that there had been a bit of a rumpus and certainly a short while afterwards Pratt, David and a rather lovely girl I've never seen before left in a great hurry, and they all looked a bit upset." She leant back in her chair and waited for Bright to write down a few brief notes.

"What time would you say the three of them left then?" he asked without looking up.

"It must have been about quarter past eleven. I can't say exactly, as we were still rather busy. Things didn't begin to quieten down until gone midnight when I managed to nip out and get some fish and chips for Joe and myself. Sam was pretty far gone by that time, as I'm sure you can imagine. In fact, he was asleep behind the bar, propped up against an empty barrel and snoring dreadfully. Joe and I carried on until about two in the morning and then we closed the bar. There were three or four people still there and they were a bit cross that we closed, but I was rather tired and I had to be in clinic at nine, so I wanted to get some sleep. We carried, or rather dragged Sam up to his room between us. We dumped him rather unceremoniously on his bed and then went our separate ways. I've no idea where Joe went, but I toddled off to my room and went straight to bed."

"So you're pretty sure that David, Jeremy and the girl never came back to the bar?"

"Well, they could have come back while the bar was still busy or when I was out getting the food, but they certainly weren't there after that."

"And the three of them had all left together at eleven fifteen?"

"Well, not together exactly," she explained. "I would say rather that Jeremy stormed out first and then David and the girl followed a few moments later."

"Thank you, Miss Warfield, you've been a great help." He stood up and moved to open the door for her.

"Oh, one more thing," he asked, "was it fairly common knowledge that David's father was a patient at the hospital?"

She hesitated slightly before answering. "Well, I don't know about common knowledge. I certainly knew and quite a few of his close friends did too, but I don't know if anyone else did. David wasn't trying to keep it quiet in any way, so anyone and everyone might have known."

"And how about Sir Edward's death? I mean, you seem to know that we're investigating it, but is that because David told you, or was it on the grapevine?"

"The grapevine, I'm afraid. If you're hoping to keep it quiet, I think you are a little bit late. It's the main topic of conversation in the hospital."

"That's a pity. Right, that really will be all then. Thank you very much."

Bright smiled at her as she left and was pleased to see her give him a very friendly smile back. He stopped to read briefly through the notes he had made and then stuck his head round the door and called for Jeremy Pratt. There were a few groans and someone blew a raspberry as a smallish young man with a round, cherubic face and very pink cheeks made his way over to Bright.

"Right, if you could just start from the time you entered the bar. Tell me exactly what happened and try not to leave anything out," Bright said, once they were settled.

"Well, it's all rather hazy, you know. I'm not sure that I can remember it all, at least not in the correct sequence, if you see what I mean."

"If you could just do the best you can, sir, it would be of considerable assistance.

"Of course, yes, I'll do the best I can." He seemed slightly embarrassed and tried to cover this by being chummy. "To tell you the truth I made rather an ass of myself that night. Over a wench, don't you know."

"A wench?" Bright queried with a deadpan expression.

"Yes, you know a girl, lady, member of the fairer sex and all that."

"I see. So what exactly happened?" he persisted.

"Um, I came into the bar at about eleven o'clock. Actually, I'd been in the pub all evening because Patty had refused to come out with me that night. It seems that David had twisted her arm and practically cornered the poor girl into agreeing to meet him after the film. She's too soft you know, can't tell a fellow when to get off. Anyway, I decided to go over to the bar to confront him and rescue Patty. Bit silly I suppose. I arrived at about eleven, as I said, found out where David was and charged straight over to him. I told him what I thought of him, trying to steal a chap's girl and all that, and he had the nerve to laugh. I mean, what's a chap supposed to do? He said that Patty had far too much taste to go out with someone like me and that I should go and get lost, or words to that effect. Anyway, I hit him and there was a bit of a scuffle until several people pulled us part. The scene had obviously distressed Patty, so I decided to leave and take it up with David at a later date, when we were alone. I obviously haven't had the chance to do that yet due to his bereavement."

"At what time did you actually leave, and did you notice if David left before, at the same time or later? And was Patty still with him?" Bright asked.

"I think I left about a quarter past and I've no idea when David left. He and Patty were still there when I went out. I went straight up to my room and I haven't seen him since."

"What is this girl Patty's surname?"

"Well, I don't know if I should tell you that. I mean, it might cause her some distress if you go barging in and ask her a lot of questions."

Bright could stand the pretence of chivalry no longer.

"Mr Pratt, withholding information from the police is a serious offence and I'm sure you don't want to ruin your career before it's even started. Besides which, if you don't tell us, someone else will."

Pratt's brave front completely crumbled in the face of this onslaught and he was suddenly only too anxious to be helpful.

"Patty Dawson's her name. She's a first-year student nurse. Very pretty, good family. Rather a nice girl all round in fact. She lives in the old nurses' home in the East End. Room number 134, or so I believe," he added unconvincingly.

"Thank you, Mr Pratt, that will be all."

Bright heaved a sigh of relief once he was alone. Jeremy Pratt had left him feeling irritated even though it had been a worthwhile interview. He had a name that would either lead to an alibi or another suspect, but whichever happened, it had to be a help. He pulled on his moustache for a moment and then got up and went to the door. He was feeling fed up with the students. If the others were telling much the same story, then it was not really necessary for him to be around for the rest of the interviews.

Dingwall had just finished with a student, so Bright went in and asked him what they were saying. It seemed that those who were able to remember were all basically saying the same, although they managed to put Pratt in a worse light than even he himself had done. Almost half the students had already been interviewed so Bright decided that they would leave the rest to the two constables and go in search of Patty Dawson.

As they reached the door, the dean came in and stopped them.

"I'm so sorry not to have been here to meet you earlier. I hope Bruno has seen to it that you have everything you require?"

"Yes, indeed, thank you," Bright answered and looked at the unruly group of medical students still waiting to be interviewed.

"Good, good," the dean said absently. "I hope you won't be too hard on them. I know that you will perhaps be a little shocked that people, so soon to be in very responsible positions, should act so irresponsibly. I beg you to remember the tremendous pressures which force them to grow up too fast. They have to come to terms with death very quickly and this tends to lead to a certain degree of hard living in an attempt to forget or at least to live with it." He ambled off in the direction of the gentlemen's lavatories, smiling benignly at all his students as he went.

"Now that's a very acute old codger, Dingwall," Bright commented. "He may indulge them all a bit, but he doesn't miss much, I'll bet. Come on, we'll have to get a move on if we're going to get back for the evening briefing."

The Central London Hospital had been a workhouse at the beginning of its chequered career and was ending it as a nurses' home. There were bars at the windows and it needed more than just a new coat of paint. Most of the rooms had no electricity sockets and much of the time there was no hot water. The local council had recently declared it unfit for habitation and the nurses were being moved to new lodgings as quickly as possible.

When the porter answered Bright's knock at the door, he was reluctant to let them in, and even less happy when he discovered that Nurse Dawson lived on the top floor.

He was an old man who walked with a stoop, wearing a baggy cardigan and bedroom slippers in addition to his uniform. He left Bright and Dingwall in a spartan room euphemistically called the "nurses' sitting room" and shuffled off up the stairs. The chairs in the sitting room seemed hardly safe enough for their intended purpose, but Bright decided to risk one anyway and he sat down in the least battered. It was surprisingly comfortable and coupled with the heat from the old electric fire, he felt suddenly tired and perhaps even a little old. He closed his eyes and tried to let the tension of the last two days slowly ebb away.

He was disturbed from his relaxation by the sound of footsteps approaching to the unmistakeable accompaniment of two people arguing. David Ellis came storming into the room only just ahead of an extremely pretty young girl.

"How did you find out about Patty?" David fumed. "Who told you I would be here? I won't have you dragging her into all this."

"Leave it out, sunshine. I've been playing 'Chase The Lady' all evening, hindered by chivalry from all sides, and I've had it up to here." Bright was suddenly angry and it stopped David short. They stood there, glowering at each other, until the girl gently touched David's arm and turned to Bright to explain.

"David's just being a bit over-protective. He doesn't think women can cope with worldly problems, but that's just ridiculous in this day and age."

"Quite right, Miss Dawson. So if you could just give us a full account of what you were doing Monday night, DC Dingwall here will make a note of it. I have this weird idea that you can clear up at least one loose end for us."

"I hope I can, Inspector. It is Inspector, isn't it?" she asked Bright and he nodded his agreement.

"I went to the film show at the medical school and met David in the bar afterwards. I was being pestered by a creep called Jeremy, so we left early. I don't know exactly what time that was, but we went to David's room and I stayed the night there with David. So you see, it's quite simple really, he has a complete alibi, but was too much of a gentleman to use it." She gave David a devoted look from under her lashes and reached out for his hand.

"Did he leave you for any length of time?" Bright asked.

"Only for a minute or two, to visit the bathroom."

"I'm sorry to have involved you in anything so sordid, Patty." David gave her hand a squeeze. "You're taking it all so well."

"Nursing isn't exactly a sheltered profession," she said with a slight laugh, "and I'm sure the inspector has heard that girls do sometimes stay the night with their boyfriends."

"Yes, indeed. And are there any witnesses to the fact that you stayed the night?" asked Bright.

"Yes," said David with a surprised look. "There is actually. You see, I know the night sister who was on duty – not very well, but enough for her to know that Sir Edward was my father. She knew I lived in the medical school and came up and knocked on my door at about two in the morning when she had a break. She wanted to tell me that my father had died, and she must have heard Patty asking who was at the door."

"How would she know what room you were in?" Bright asked innocently.

"I would have thought that as she's been around a bit, she probably knows there is a list of the room allocations in Bruno's cubby hole. She could quite easily have looked me up," David hastily explained.

"I presume your stepmother was contacted as next of kin then?"

"Yes, she was telephoned as soon as my father was certified dead, about half past one or so. She didn't come in, but I went over after I had been told and said goodbye, if you see what I mean." He seemed slightly embarrassed but Bright was much too interested to notice.

"So, you actually saw the body soon afterwards, then? Why didn't you tell me this before?"

"You didn't ask me, and to tell you the truth, I hadn't really thought about it in that way."

"Did you notice anything amiss?" Bright asked hopefully but then added in a more pessimistic tone, "I expect the nurses had cleared everything up by the time you got there?"

"Not everything, Inspector. You see, as this was a case of sudden death, all the drip tubing and things like that were left and my father was not laid out. It's normal procedure, you see – they want everything left untouched until the post-mortem has been done."

"Do you mean to say that all the syringes and things were still there and will have been kept?"

"No, nothing extraneous, just the things attached to the body. All the resus equipment was cleared away long before I arrived."

"Oh well, it was just a thought, Mr Ellis. You might have noticed something odd if it had still been around, but on the other hand, no one else did."

"I'm afraid not, Inspector."

"Right, then I think we have all we need from Miss Dawson and also from you, Mr Ellis. Please remember, for future reference, that when you lied, you failed to protect Miss Dawson but you did cause us a lot of unnecessary hassle."

David had the good grace to look genuinely sorry as Bright left and went out into the cold night air with Dingwall.

"You know I have this theory, Dingwall, that all little, pretty blondes are in reality as hard as nails, and I don't think that Patty Dawson is going to be the exception that proves the rule. She's so hard, you probably couldn't scratch her with a diamond."

When Bright went in to the incident room, Sergeant Harper and a team of assistants were feverishly typing all the reports into the computer as quickly as they arrived. This was done every morning and evening, the rest of the day being spent asking the computer to search out links or discrepancies in the information fed into it.

The evening briefing was a fairly informal affair and once everyone had arrived and settled themselves on the desks and chairs, Bright started the proceedings.

"Right, Hoppy, what news on the hospital front?"

"Well, I have here two rather interesting initial-action interviews, guv." He looked at the two sheets of paper in front of him. "One of the night sisters says she nipped over to the medical school to let David know that his father had died and she heard a girl's voice coming from the room. And this one is from a student nurse who says a fellow student, one Patty Dawson, was in the habit of staying the night with David in his room at the medical school. I've got all her particulars down here."

"Thanks, Hoppy. I don't want to take the wind out of your sails but we already have them. A medical student told us all about it. We have also confirmed it with Miss Dawson and David Ellis himself, so it checks out all round now. Anything else of interest turn up?"

"Poor Denison, the SOC officer, has had one hell of a day, guv. First of all, he was given the drip tubing and bits that had been attached to the body at the time of death. He was hopeful of at least one unexplained or out-of-place print somewhere on it, but the whole lot had been handled by the crash team, the pathologists, the porters shifting the body, Uncle Tom Cobley and all. The one and only print clearly on the tubing actually belongs to the mortuary attendant. Anyway, severely disappointed though he was, he decided to press on with fingerprinting members of the hospital staff. However, he got told, in no uncertain terms, that members of one of the unions – NUPE, I think it is – have been advised not to give their prints until they have received assurances that the prints will be destroyed after use and not held on record for future reference. Denison tried to reassure them that the prints would be destroyed but they won't take his word for it. I went along to see their shop steward but he wasn't impressed by me, either. I think he's worried some of his members might have records under other names or something, not that we have the time to check them all out, right now. So, what do you want to do about that one, guv?"

Bright sighed and ran his hand through his short hair. "I could really do without some awkward bastard holding up the whole investigation." He thought for a moment. "I think it would probably be best if I ask the super to speak to the shop steward himself. He's waiting for me to go up and give him a progress report as soon as we've finished here, so I'll mention it then."

"If you don't mind me saying so, guv," Hoppy continued tentatively, "it doesn't help that they think we're investigating a series of minor crimes around the hospital. I mean, they all think we're going to nail 'em for pilfering hospital cutlery or smoking grass in the porters' rest room."

"Point taken, Hoppy, but I think we should try to keep it quiet for a little while longer."

"Yes, well, on that score, I think I should tell you something else, guv."

"I'm not sure that I can take any more bad news tonight, Hoppy."

"Sorry, guv," Hoppy said.

He was then silent for a few moments until Bright stood up impatiently and said, "Go on, go on, don't keep me in suspense. What's happened?"

"One of the nurses mentioned that a gentleman of the press has been hanging around asking questions about the mini crime wave that the hospital is supposed to be suffering. He was asking for specific instances, but she was unable to help him, and he also wanted to know exactly how many policemen were involved in the investigation."

"Shit! That's all we bloody well need, Hoppy. You know how quickly those bastards breed. There may only have been one today but there will be fifteen tomorrow."

"Cheer up. I mean, the inquest's the day after tomorrow and that would have let the cat out of the bag anyway."

"I know that, Hoppy, but I had hoped for just one more day's grace."

He turned to Sergeant Harper. "You'd better get on to Chelsea and warn them that the press is getting on the trail. They'll have to step up the watch on the Ellis family home. Right, well that leads us neatly on to the house-to-house enquiries around the homes of Julian Penfold and Margaret Swainson. What have you got for us there, Slim?"

"Not a lot, as it happens, guv." He shifted his considerable weight into a more comfortable position. "As you suspected, most of the inhabitants were out at work all day, but if you'll let me have a couple more helpers I'll go back and start again."

"You mean you didn't get anything at all?"

Slim consulted his notebook and listed his day's achievements.

"We interviewed six assorted elderly people, all of whom were stone deaf; one Bangladeshi Lady, who spoke no English; and fifteen small children, all of whom were asleep during the relative times. Upper Street nick are still trying to locate the lads who were on that beat the night before last. Unfortunately, they both went on days off yesterday."

"Terrific. You'd better take a couple of helpers and get back on the job then, Slim."

Bright watched as he levered himself out of the chair, beckoned to two of the night-shift constables and left to continue his search for an observant neighbour.

"Right, Sergeant Jameson." Bright turned to the officer in charge of the night shift. "I want some of your men to carry on at the hospital and some more patrolling the area and interviewing passers-by. We've got to build up a picture of who was around and about that night."

"Yes, sir, I'll sort that out."

"Okay. I'm off then. See you in the morning. Are you coming, Hoppy?"

"Yes, guv. Haven't you forgotten the super, though?"

"Bugger it. Yes I had. Well off you go. I'd better go and see the old man.

Hoppy shook his head as Bright disappeared along the corridor.

"He really loves these messy cases, he does," he said to Sergeant Jameson. "Me, I prefer something more straightforward, like one young thug kicking another's head in, or a little old lady getting mugged." With this cryptic remark Hoppy went home.

Chapter 6

While Bright waited for the hospital administrator to arrive at his office, he turned the question of the syringe over in his mind and tried to picture the injection area on the ward. Try as he might, he could not remember seeing a very large syringe. It would have to have been an extremely large one to hold more than twenty millilitres, as the pathologist said had been used. If the large syringes were in constant use they would be found in the injection area, but if they were rarely used, they would probably be kept in the store room. Bright knew that it would be a tremendous help if they could find the murder weapon, but it would be like looking for one particular piece of hay in a haystack. It might not even be a large syringe; the murderer might have refilled a small one or used two, or Dr Hull and the coroner could have been mistaken about the volume of air involved. There were so many possibilities. Using two syringes or refilling the one would be clumsy; it would be much safer to use one big one. As for the experts being wrong, it was so rare for two doctors to agree that when it happened, Bright felt honour-bound to believe them.

He looked at his watch impatiently. "Where has that man got to?" he murmured to himself, and then explained to the startled secretary, "It's ten past nine and he might not start work until the afternoon, but I've got to get the rubbish sifting under way as soon as possible or we'll be doing it all night." He tapped his fingers on the desk top and hummed tunelessly to himself. "Is he usually this late?"

Before she could reply, however, the administrator entered the room.

"Hello, Inspector. Sorry to keep you waiting – the traffic was appalling. But I don't suppose you've come about that. What can I do for you?"

Bright came straight to the point. "I understand that due to action taken by the portering staff, no rubbish has been burnt for the past few days."

"That is correct, yes. It was in fact early on Tuesday that a porter was injured by a needle in a rubbish bag and nothing has been shifted since."

"Does that often happen?"

"Not really. The nursing staff are all aware of the dangers and use the special sharps disposal bins, but obviously an occasional needle goes astray." He sat down behind the cluttered desk and indicated that Bright should take the chair opposite.

"How often are the rubbish bags collected?"

"Six in the morning and six in the evening, daily."

"So, the Monday-night rubbish is sitting out there just waiting for us to find it," Bright said with a smile. "I'm sorry but we're going to have to search through it. I have a team ready to sort through the bags and thought perhaps you might want to check up on them. You know, make sure they're not making too much of a mess or anything."

"I'm sure they couldn't make more of a mess than there already is, Inspector," the administrator replied ruefully.

"There is just one thing more," Bright continued. "Do you use any syringes larger than twenty millilitres?"

"We use a lot of fifty-mill bladder syringes, but they have a different end which can't be attached to a needle or a drip – it's much too wide. The large syringes that can be used in that way are very rare. We don't give our patients many injections that size. More in a vet's line, I should think. Of course, we do keep a few of them around, especially on the oncology and endocrinology wards; a general surgery ward might keep one or two in stock but probably don't use them too often. At a rough guess I'd say we only use about ten a month throughout the whole hospital. If you'd like to come with me to one of the wards, I'll get someone to show you."

Bright thanked him profusely and later, when he walked quickly around to the back of the hospital and the rubbish dump, he was clutching an enormous syringe. A rather dejected group of overalled and gloved young policemen stood ready to start their unpleasant task.

"Right," Bright began his briefing. "I want you to look for anything unusual. I know that doesn't mean much, but if you don't think it should be there, keep it. Specifically, you are looking for a doctor's white coat or some other disguise – overalls, theatre garb, anything like that. Sergeant Hopwood's got a few examples over there for you to look at, if you haven't already done so. I want all the gloves, and there will be hundreds of them, and also any fifty-mill syringes, like the one I have here, with or without needles attached. When you find one of these, I not only want you to keep the syringe but also all the surrounding rubbish. Right, well, off you go then."

He stepped back and watched as some of the policemen began opening rubbish bags and tipping them out onto a huge plastic sheet, while others sifted through it and put the discarded muck into other bags. There was no reason for Bright to stand around watching them, so he decided to go and try to see a few of the people who had said something interesting in their first interviews. He tackled Nurse Jensen, the junior student, first. She was a rather sulky girl.

"You'd better come in, I suppose," she said unhelpfully and then continued, "I do wish you could have left it till later. I mean, I've only just woken up and you can't expect me to have got myself together yet."

"I'm sorry, but it is rather important," he explained.

She flopped down on the unmade bed and it seemed to Bright that both she and the bed wobbled for a second or two like an enormous jelly.

"I want you to tell me what happened that night in your own words. You never know, you might have missed some little thing and it could be important."

"You don't have to give me all that, I know you're here hoping to catch me out in a lie. I know nobody believes that I saw Dr Cawthorne at eleven thirty, but I did. And I put up that drip before he gave his injection, so there. You don't have to believe me and I know you probably won't, because he's a doctor and I'm only a nurse. You know, that doesn't mean he's more likely to tell the truth. He's less likely to in fact, because he has more to lose. It's so unfair."

"Now I'm not saying that I don't believe you," Bright began in a conciliatory tone of voice, "but I want you to realise just how serious an offence it is to mislead the police, especially in a case of murder. I want you to think carefully and then tell me the absolute truth about those two incidents." He had wanted to frighten her into honesty but there was an obstinate line to her mouth which told him that he had not been completely successful.

"You're all the same, you men. I know I'm not too pretty and I know I'm not too clever but that doesn't mean I'm untrustworthy. I'm better than Dr Cawthorne. Why don't you go and do a little digging into his past. You'll find that the same thing has happened before," she said spitefully.

"Hold on, that's a very serious accusation. You could land Dr Cawthorne in a lot of trouble if it's true."

"He doesn't care how much trouble he lands me in," she continued. "He's just trying to cover up that he forgot to flush through his injection. He's frightened he might get a slap on the wrist. A mistake like that from a nurse would probably mean instant dismissal, but they all get together and hush things up when it's a doctor."

Bright was interested to note that she was far more concerned about the drip than the alleged sighting of the doctor. She probably had not grasped the fact that if Dr Cawthorne went into the room that late, it did not matter when the bag had been changed, and it was definitely the bag-changing incident that worried her most.

It makes me think that she's telling the truth about seeing him, but lying through her teeth about the bag. But that just doesn't make sense, Bright thought as he made his way back through the now familiar passages, back to see Hoppy and his intrepid team of rubbish sorters.

"Got anything?" he asked with unusual brevity.

"Not a lot, but we've put it over here for you, anyway." Hoppy indicated a small pile of odds and ends and a much larger heap of assorted plastic gloves. Bright had not expected anything to turn up early in the search because they would have to look through Wednesday's and Thursday's rubbish before they reached the all-important Tuesday-morning contribution. Hoppy was standing and looking at the finds disgustedly.

"There are eight fifty-mill syringes here, but they're all those ones with wide necks for bladder washouts. The rest of this stuff is what was with the syringes but is all pretty much what you would expect." Hoppy was clearly more than a little bored by his mornings work.

"How do you know what to expect?" Bright asked. "'Old up, when you was in hospital last year, that was your prostate, wasn't it? So I suppose you do know all about bladder washouts and gory stuff like that. I hadn't realised

I'd asked an expert to watch over the lads," he teased. Hoppy looked embarrassed as one of the young constables snorted with suppressed laughter.

"Don't you laugh, my lad," Hoppy told him. "One day you'll be middle-aged and unable to pee and then you won't laugh. We'll see what you think about bladder washouts then, won't we?"

The constable looked suitably abashed and stared intently at the great pile of filthy, bloodstained rubbish that had just been tipped out in front of him. He half-heartedly went to turn some of it over but then suddenly stopped and reached out to pick something up. Hoppy and Bright had not been paying much attention to the work going on but the deliberate way in which his hand moved and the surprised look on his face caught their attention. They moved closer and looked at the large and unmistakeable article.

"A piece of hard evidence at last, Hoppy," Bright said. He could hardly stop himself from jumping up and down in his excitement. "Oh Hoppy, even if we find nothing else, the rubbish-sifting has been worthwhile. We have here something that even the densest of prosecuting counsels will understand. Something no jury can ignore even if the defence does call it a coincidence. A doctor's coat, Hoppy, in the rubbish bins. It reeks of disguise and dastardly deeds in the night. Exhibit A, my lord, is one plain white, medium size doctor's coat with no identifying marks except... Well, well, well. What have we here?" Bright very carefully smoothed out the tatty name tape sewn inside the collar of the coat, doing his best to touch it as little as possible.

" 'Dr C. Cawthorne,' " he read and was silent for a moment or two. He was holding the grubby coat delicately with one hand and stroking his beard with his other hand. "That stupid geezer ought to take more care of his possessions. You see what happens if you're careless and leave things lying about – you end up chief suspect."

He threw the evidence into the plastic bag the constable was holding and gestured towards it.

"Seal it, label it and send it to forensic," he said as he headed in the direction of the main hospital, calling over his shoulder, "I'll be back later," and he disappeared around the corner.

* * *

Dr Cawthorne's nerves were obviously not standing up to the strain. He was constantly fidgeting, shifting his weight from one foot to the other, and he seemed unable to keep his hands still.

"I don't know why you want to ask me more questions, Inspector. I told the constable absolutely everything and he wrote it all down."

"Yes, I know, Doctor, but one or two other things have cropped up and I need to ask you about them."

"I'm a very busy man, Inspector," he said, adjusting the stethoscope hanging around his neck. "So, can we get this over with? This clinic starts in ten minutes."

"Well then, Doctor, it's in your best interest to assist us in solving this problem as quickly as possible. The sooner we catch the culprit, the sooner you will be left alone, won't you?"

"Of course, I shall assist you to the best of my ability." Dr Cawthorne might have sounded pompous if he had not been so anxious.

"I'm very glad to hear it, Doctor. You have no idea the problems we have with people who are so busy hiding their past misdemeanours and generally covering things up that they finish by not being helpful at all."

"I don't know what you mean, Inspector," Dr Cawthorne said defensively. "I haven't covered anything up. I haven't got anything to be ashamed about, and I assure you that I did not come back to the ward later. I was very busy on another ward. Nurse Johnson on Edith Cavell Ward will confirm that I was with a patient there most of the evening. She'll corroborate my story." He took a clean handkerchief from his pocket and mopped his brow.

"Now, now, Doctor. Don't get upset. I didn't mean anything by it," Bright reassured him "We'll check with Nurse Johnson, but I'm sure she will confirm your whereabouts. I just want to be sure about this drip. You can be honest with me. I don't care if you should have flushed it through or not, or whatever it is that's worrying you. It wasn't the cause of death, so all I want to know is, was it a new bag or not? You see, it's vital for us to get all the timing right."

"The bag was almost through, I promise you." He seemed desperate to be believed. "Look, I'll admit that I didn't mention it to Julie, Nurse Banks that is, and I persuaded her to tell you that I did, but I had to convince you, because it's true. I don't know what that little first year is up to, but I really and honestly can assure you that the bag was nearly through when I gave him the cimetidine."

He certainly seemed sincere and Bright was tempted to believe him. There was something in the desperation of his last speech that was very convincing.

A nurse hurried into the cubicle where they were talking and apologised. "I was just going to get things ready for the first patient," she explained.

"We won't be a minute, love," Bright said and, when she had left, turned once again to Dr Cawthorne. "Just one more thing. Have you, by any chance, lost one of your white coats?"

"Good Lord, I've absolutely no idea." He seemed genuinely surprised. "Why, have you found one?"

"Yes, it was found amongst the rubbish that we have been looking through this morning."

"Well, I've no idea how it got there," Dr Cawthorne said firmly. "We all drive the linen lady wild because we're always losing our white coats. I'm sure I've never thrown one away, but God alone knows what does happen to the ones I lose. Now, if you don't mind, I have patients waiting. If there is anything more you want to know, perhaps you could come back later?"

"Yes, I think that will be all for the moment, Dr Cawthorne. Thank you for your co-operation."

Bright walked along the imposing corridors of the old part of the hospital and found himself once again at the back.

"I didn't mean to come back and see you so soon, Hoppy, but I got lost. Still, as I'm here, I might as well see how you're getting on."

"We've got several more bladder syringes, but we also have two proper ones for you to see." He led Bright over to a few items laid out on a small plastic sheet and kept separately from the rest of the finds. "We've kept everything that was with them as well, although it's nothing spectacular. One's got a needle attached but the other is on its tod."

Bright looked at the mess of bloody swabs, tubing, crumpled paper and surgeons' gloves. "Apart from the dead flowers, I want everything that can be fingerprinted, done. I somehow doubt they'll find anything, but it still has to be done. The surgeons' gloves are the best bet. How much longer before you've finished here?" he asked.

"It won't take long now," Hoppy replied and then pointed at the two syringes. "I don't know if you noticed, but they're not identical. Look, one has blue markings and the other has black."

"So they have," Bright said with interest. "How very observant of you, Hoppy. Right, get them fingerprinted pronto and then we'll take them up to the administrator before sending them to forensics. We'll hold an identification parade of syringes. Now, how come it never occurred to a genius like me that the syringe might not have come from this hospital?" he asked nobody in particular. "I suppose because it's such an obvious place to find a syringe that it would seem silly to get one elsewhere. Like bringing coals to Newcastle or ice to the South Pole. Mind you, we'll probably find that they use all sorts of syringes here and that will be that, but if they don't, Hoppy, if one of these syringes came in from outside, it must be the murder weapon. It must have been murder and we've got a lead. I never realised there was so much to know about syringes before. I can see I shall have to make a study of them and write a treatise on them, or lecture police cadets for hours and hours and make them more bored than they've ever been before."

While he waited for the fingerprinting to be done, Bright told his sergeant that he had got hold of the night sister's home telephone number and given her a call on his way back from Nurse Jensen.

"She confirmed that she had rung Lady Ellis about half past one. The phone was picked up very promptly but the dragon might have one beside her bed, so we will have to check. The Night Sister then went over to tell David as she said. He took some time to rouse, and he was only wearing a towelling robe when he answered the door. She also heard a girl's voice asking who it was, so that seems to be holding up all right. Have you finished? Good, pop 'em in separate bags and we'll take them with us. Did you find anything?" he asked Denison, the SOC officer.

"On the syringe without a needle, we've got some very clear prints, which on the whole don't match any of the suspects, but I'll have to compare the photos back at the lab. No prints on the other syringe, not even a smear. By the way, had you noticed that it looks a bit old and tatty, as if it's been used several times? I'll have to ship all this other stuff back to the lab as well. I can't mess about here trying to find fingerprints inside rubber gloves. It's much too tricky. I'll let you have a full report tomorrow."

"Guv!" One of the overalled constables called, and as Bright looked at him, he nodded towards a man standing at the corner, scribbling in a notebook.

"Bugger it," Bright said and walked briskly over to the intruder. The rubbish sifters all paused in their work to watch.

"Can I help?" Bright asked more aggressively than politely.

The man flashed a press card and asked, "Perhaps you could tell me what exactly is it that you are doing here?"

"I think that's fairly obvious, don't you? We're looking through the rubbish."

"You're looking for evidence?"

"We're certainly not doing it for our health." Bright gave him a cool smile and tried to turn away.

"Is it to do with the crime wave that the hospital has been experiencing lately?"

"That's right, sir."

"So what exactly are you looking for?" the reporter persisted.

"This and that, anything odd. You know the sort of thing." Unwilling to lie and even less willing to tell the truth, Bright opted for evasiveness.

"What sort of things would that be? Handbags, purses and wallets?" the reporter answered himself, and Bright readily agreed.

"Yes, indeed, anything of that sort."

"You seem to have an awful lot of men involved in what is, after all, an investigation into a relatively minor problem."

"I'm shocked to hear that you think this a relatively minor problem, sir. You blokes are always calling us uncaring, but here we are to protect and help the old, the sick and the poor nurses and you dare to criticise us for that, too. We can't win, can we?"

Temporarily silenced, but not totally convinced, the journalist left. Bright collected the syringes and took Hoppy to the administration block.

"Do you think we're likely to find a pair of gloves with prints in, guv?" Hoppy asked.

"Not really," Bright answered. "When you think about it, Hoppy, we're not dealing with your average dumbo. This geezer does not take any chances. I'd lay odds that he did use gloves but he won't have thrown them away with the syringe. It will probably be six months after we've both retired when they finally finish dusting all these gloves for prints, and even then, they'll only find a pair with David's prints on and he'll be able to argue that he used them legitimately."

When they reached the office, the administrator had already left but Bright was determined to get the problem of the syringe settled at once.

"He should not have left the hospital while we were still checking the rubbish. It was his duty to stay," Bright explained as they waited for the man to reach home so that he could be called back to work.

When he returned, the administrator checked the files, muttering crossly to himself about having had to battle through the rush-hour traffic twice.

"You're lucky you found something with that rubbish sifting," Hoppy said quietly to Bright. "Otherwise I think the lads would have lynched you."

"Luck had nothing to do with it, Hoppy. I admit that I didn't expect to find the white coat, it would have been just as inconspicuous for the murderer to have left it on a chair or something, but the syringe is different. You know the first instinct of the murderer is to get rid of the murder weapon. They know if they are caught with it, it's curtains. Nine times out of ten they ditch it within a few yards of the scene of the crime and usually that's the way we catch them. You know that the slow, meticulous and often unpleasant search, while being boring and unglamorous, is probably the most productive aspect of our work. Searches, and house-to-house inquiries – now they really are boring. All right, I admit that I didn't know that the murderer would use a spare white coat, a fifty-mill syringe and wear gloves, but it seemed likely. Just as it seems unlikely that he wandered away afterwards with all those things tucked under his arm. Ergo – that's Latin Hoppy, you didn't know I'd been studying that as well, did you? Ergo, he had to dump the doings somewhere, so why not three different rubbish bins as he passes them on his way out? It's logic, innit?"

Bright grinned at Hoppy who was about to reply when the administrator interrupted.

"Ah, here we are. We use two different syringe firms."

Bright groaned but the administrator continued, "Rosslyn supply us with one-, two-, five-, ten- and twenty-mill syringes and the fifty-mill bladder syringes. Barkworth's supply us with insulin syringes, and twenty- and fifty-mill ordinary ones too. Now let's see." He reached out a hand towards the two plastic bags but stopped and looked questioningly at Bright before touching them. "May I?" he asked.

"Yes, of course. We've finished with them for the moment, but please don't take them out of the bags."

The administrator inspected them both carefully.

"This one marked in blue, without a needle, is the one made by Barkworth's. The one in black I've not seen before."

He flipped through his file on syringes and muttered to himself again.

"No, no, it's not Downe's – they have a funny logo with a staff and snake like the BMA. And it doesn't look like IDOR either. Wait a moment. Yes, here it is." He pointed to a page at the head of which was a large B inside a circle which itself was inside a square. A similar design was on the syringe.

"It's Burns. Well, I can tell you straight away that we have never dealt with them here. In fact, the area health authority don't either. I don't know of any NHS hospital that would use them because, although their equipment is excellent, it is rather expensive."

Bright picked up the bag containing the alien syringe and looked at it admiringly. "Our first real lead, Hoppy. It may not look much but it's our first real lead. Let's just hope that it leads us somewhere other than a dead end."

He turned to the administrator and asked hopefully, "What about the needle? Anything special about that?"

"No, there is one firm that is outstanding at making those and they don't have much competition at all in this country. We certainly use them and, off-hand, I don't know of anywhere that doesn't, although I'm sure there must be some."

"Oh well, you can't have everything." Bright was philosophical rather than disappointed. "It would have been nice to have a rare needle with a rare syringe and only one place in the country that uses them both, but no case is perfect. Thanks for all your help and I'm really sorry to have called you back from home. We'll get cracking on tracing the syringe first thing in the morning."

The administrator refrained from pointing out that he could have told them about the syringe first thing in the morning, too, if they were not going to start to trace it straight away.

"Before you go, Inspector," he said as Bright and Hoppy stood up to leave. "I did mean to see you earlier anyway, but it slipped my mind."

"What can I do for you?"

"We seem to be developing a bit of a press problem and I wanted your advice as to how we should handle it."

Bright sat down again and pulled a face. "I appreciate your problem, but on the whole it is one that the hospital is just going to have to live through, and it's going to get worse. What have you done about it so far?"

"Oh Lord," the administrator said in despair, "I've tried being evasive, I've talked about thefts and muggings and even hinted at sexual assaults upon student nurses, but I'm not sure that I convinced them. There's the inquest tomorrow morning anyway and it's not going to take them long to put two and two together after that and we'll be inundated. I mean, I'm having difficulty with just a few of them around. What will it be like tomorrow when I'm falling over them the whole time?"

"Look, I'll give you a few suggestions. Do you remember that bloke who was the spokesman or whatever during the Falklands Crisis? Take a leaf out of his book – say as little as you can, as rarely as you can and as late as you can; and if they really press you, say it all again but slower." He loosened his tie and slumped back in his chair. "If the press quickly catch on to what's happened, the super will be giving a press conference tomorrow at five o'clock, presumably so that he can get himself on the six o'clock news, but if by some chance they haven't realised that Sir Edward was murdered in his hospital bed, he'll put if off until they do. I'll be keeping in touch with you during the day to monitor the situation but you will probably have to issue some sort of a non-statement tomorrow afternoon or evening."

"Right, I'll work on something just in case." The administrator seemed a little anxious and fiddled with a pen on his desk. "What happens if they really start to get in the way? I mean, can we expect any help from you to get rid of them?"

"Not unless they commit a crime, I'm afraid, sir. As you know, trespass is a civil offence, so we can't forcefully remove them or arrest them, and whereas with a lot of people you could use us as a threat or a bluff, reporters will know their rights. There's no way they will let you get away with threatening to have them arrested. Your best bet is to just ignore them until they get bored, but that may take quite a while."

The administrator sighed and thanked Bright for his help. Once the press had got their teeth into the story, he would get no peace, so he went home to prepare himself for the next day.

Before going back for the evening briefing, Bright popped in to Hailey Ward and was pleased to see that Sister was on duty again. She was concentrating hard on bringing the nursing-care cards up to date and checking her juniors' entries on them. She was frowning deeply and was visibly relieved to be distracted.

"Hello, Inspector. What can I do to help you?" She smiled and pulled forward a wooden stool for him to sit on.

"That does not look the most comfortable of seats," he commented.

"Just be thankful you're not an impoverished young nurse, catching your tights on the splinters that those things have in abundance." She laughed.

"I've never fully appreciated the problems associated with wearing tights. It's obvious that I shall have to do some research into them."

"Come now, Inspector, what's the problem?" she asked, and Bright paused for a moment.

"What I wanted to ask was, well." He fumbled for the right words. "If a drip runs through and no one notices, will air get into the bloodstream?"

Bright felt sure that it would, and expected an immediate and vehement defence of Nurse Jensen, but he was surprised to see an amused look on the sister's face.

"No, Inspector, it will not to any great degree. You see the blood in the vein is at a greater pressure than the air. However, the movement of the blood may drag a little air into the vein by suction, but the needles or cannulae that we use are small and very little will enter. Also, nowadays, all giving sets – the actual drip tubes, that is – have a little safety device to make absolutely sure. Here, let me show you."

She went over to the man in the nearest bed and pointed to a small chamber near the top of his drip.

"You see here, there is a little ball, floating on the liquid. As the chamber empties, the ball sinks and eventually covers the outlet, stopping air from going down the tube. Once the drip stops, a clot forms on the end of the cannula and a new drip may have to be sited somewhere else on the poor patient's body. That is why we don't like to let drips run through, not because of air getting in. It would be impossible for much air to get in, certainly not the amount that killed Sir Edward." She looked suddenly concerned. "I'm sorry Inspector, have I ruined your pet theory?" she asked.

"Not in the least, but I think you may have ruined Nurse Jensen's."

Chapter 7

"Do come on in, Inspector. I was wondering when it would be my turn. Officer Dingwall, so nice to see you again." Mrs Ellis turned to Bright and explained, "He was very kind when he came to question me earlier about my movements on… the night, but I expect he has told you all about our little talk and how he so very kindly helped me with the zip on my carrier bag. So awkward. It had run over the handle and got stuck. It was only one of those lightweight foldaway things, so annoying that it got stuck, but he sorted it all out for me. If you would sit down over there, Inspector." She indicated a large and comfortable-looking armchair. "And you here, Officer Dingwall." She pulled forward an upright chair. Bright smiled smugly and then grimaced as his arm chair turned out to have a broken spring on one side, making it very difficult to sit upright.

"I do hope you are both comfortable. Of course, hotels can never be quite the same as one's own home, I always think."

Bright silently agreed.

"Now, I'll just order some tea to be sent up and then we can start."

While she was telephoning reception, Bright made a series of faces, indicating to DC Dingwall just what he thought of little old ladies who didn't let you get a word in edgeways, let alone a question, and why hadn't he been warned before they arrived? Dingwall just smiled and pretended not to understand what he was trying to say. Bright gave up in disgust and looked around the room instead. It was a fairly typically impersonal hotel room, although it was large and had an area furnished as a sitting room. It was adequate and comfortable, but in no way luxurious.

Mrs Ellis seemed younger than Lady Ellis, probably in her late fifties or early sixties. *On the other hand, she could have had a face-lift and really be ninety*, Bright thought to himself. Everything about her was in impeccable taste, from the top of her beautifully coiffured silver hair to the tips of her black court shoes. She was wearing a plain black and very simple cashmere dress with only a Victorian brooch for ornament. But Bright could see that the clothes were not new and her black handbag had been mended. She had the air of a lady living off an income that had been fixed slightly lower than that to which she was accustomed. Sir Edward could not have been so generous to his first wife as Bright had been led to believe by Lady Ellis.

"There, that's all done now," she said as she came across and sat opposite Bright. "I always think talking is so much easier if you have a cup of tea. I know it's more usual to have coffee at this time of the morning but when you live abroad it is so nice to have proper tea again that it seems almost criminal to drink coffee. Not that France is so very far away from a geographical point of view, but it is certainly miles and miles away as far as customs go, and they really cannot make a decent cup of tea. I think it must be the water. Dear Edward always said I would miss England if I went to live abroad, but I must admit that it is really only the tea I miss."

"I've read the account of your interview, Mrs Ellis, but would you mind quickly going through what you said, just to refresh my memory?"

"Not at all, Inspector, although I'm quite sure that your memory doesn't need refreshing. I'll be as succinct as possible. Now, let's see. I went to dinner with some friends of mine, the Hendersons. They live in a very nice little town house in Chelsea. At about ten o'clock I decided to leave and they very kindly called me a taxi. I'm sure the cab driver will remember me because after we had gone a little way I had to ask him to return to Chelsea as I had forgotten my umbrella. I don't know what time we left the Hendersons' the second time but we arrived back here at about ten to eleven." She smiled at Bright and offered the two policemen some tea and biscuits, which had just arrived.

"Yes, it was fortunate that the Hendersons used a radio cab firm so that we were able to trace the driver quite easily," Bright said. "He confirms everything that you have told us, but it appears that he didn't actually see you enter the hotel. In fact, it seems that no one saw you come in."

"Yes, I remember, it was most unusual. In all the years that I've been coming here I've never known the desk to be left unattended so early. Anyone could have come in. It was fortunate that I had forgotten to hand in my key because otherwise I could not have got into my room. You know, several years ago, they mislaid the key to that little glass-fronted cupboard where all the room keys are kept, and they insisted on looking everywhere for it before breaking the lock to give me my key. It turned out that one of the receptionists had absentmindedly put it into her pocket and gone off duty. Such a silly girl, and we all had to wait nearly half an hour in the dining room before we could get to our rooms. Mind you, Mr Shassi very kindly gave us all a free drink while we waited."

"The desk was only left unattended for a short while, Mrs Ellis, and the receptionist seems to think that it was later than eleven o'clock."

"Perhaps she doesn't want to admit to leaving the desk too often. If it was the small, dark, and rather flirtatious young lady on duty, then she quite often goes and talks to the barman. She can see the desk from the end of the bar, you see, but she might have gone further into the room. Or perhaps she had nipped out to the lavatory. She wasn't there, Inspector. I don't know why, but she wasn't there."

"We'll look into it again, Mrs Ellis. Now, did you go and see Sir Edward while he was in hospital?"

"No, I had no idea that he was ill at all," she said with a vehement shake of her head. "If I had known, I certainly would have popped in to see him. I always think that hospitals are such dreary places and you must have lots and lots of visitors to cheer it up. I could have taken him all sorts of little delicacies such as caviar and truffles. I always used to tempt him with things like that when he had a tummy upset."

Bright thought that if he were feeling ill, caviar and truffles would be well down on his list of tempting delicacies. Mrs Ellis was looking wistfully out of the window, probably thinking of far-off days and distant sick beds. Bright cleared his throat noisily.

"Oh, I'm so sorry, I was just thinking…" She made a little deprecating gesture with her hands. "Well, it doesn't matter what I was thinking, but I'm sure you must have more questions to ask?"

"Did any of your family know that you were in London, Mrs Ellis?" Bright continued.

"I'm not really sure, Inspector." She paused for a moment's thought. "I don't think that I actually let any of them know; somehow I seem to have been terribly rushed just recently and it completely slipped my mind," she explained. "Anyway, I wasn't planning to stay here long and I had so much to do and the children would have been dreadfully upset if they knew that I had been in London but had not had time to see them. No, that's not true." She stopped with a shake of her head and gave Bright a rather sad smile. "I'll be honest, Inspector. I have little in common with my two children now and I don't often tell them I am in England because I have little desire to see them and I am sure that they have no desire to see me."

"I understand, Mrs Ellis. So, how often would you say you come to London?"

"Oh, two or three times a year, I should think," she said, and then added in a more confidential tone, "I'm a rather erratic person, I'm afraid, Inspector, and so it varies depending on how I feel. I see your cup is empty. Do let me pour you some more tea."

"When exactly was your last trip? Yes, three sugars, thank you." He put the cup on a small table beside him and refused a biscuit. Mrs Ellis fussed over Dingwall and checked that he was still drinking his tea and then started to fiddle with the things on the tray. "When exactly was your last trip to London?" persisted Bright.

"I really can't remember exactly, Inspector; it was several months ago, anyway. I don't wish to seem inquisitive, and I'm sure you have a very good reason, but why are you asking all these questions about my trips to London? I fail to see quite why they should have any bearing on the case." She smiled at Bright and put her head slightly on one side.

"Because you seem anxious that I shouldn't probe into these visits, Mrs Ellis," Bright admitted candidly.

She looked faintly discomfited for a moment, but then she gave him a rueful smile. "Is it so obvious? Goodness, I am glad I'm not the murderer if I am so transparent to you, Inspector. I shall have to be more honest with you." She stood up and walked over to the window. It was a grey and damp day. A steady drizzle had made the rooftops and pavements glisten and drops of water slowly trickled down the window pane.

"I have been coming here for ten days every other month since last August. I spend the first three days as an inpatient at the Nuffield Clinic and the next five days continuing my treatment as an outpatient. I have a couple more days staying here recuperating and then I return to France."

She turned to Bright and explained, "I have cancer you see, Inspector, and I am undergoing a new form of treatment that is unavailable in France at the moment."

"I'm very sorry, Mrs Ellis. Well, the explanation seems quite satisfactory, and we can check it quite easily. Perhaps we can move on now to some other little points I wanted to clear up?" He looked inquiringly at Mrs Ellis, who nodded. "What exactly were your relations with Sir Edward?" He asked.

"I'm sorry, I don't understand the question?" She looked rather puzzled, and Dingwall seemed a bit mystified as well.

"Perhaps I should have been clearer," Bright agreed. "What has been the nature of your contact with Sir Edward in recent months? Have you had any contact at all? If so, was it of a friendly nature or purely business? Or perhaps your only contact has been through solicitors?"

"Oh, I see what you mean, Inspector. Well, I had very little contact with Edward at all. It was indeed mainly done through solicitors. They worked out the financial side of things, you understand." She waved her hand in a rather vague manner. "The divorce settlement and suchlike was settled some time ago. Of course my solicitors were in touch with his from time to time, about the villa in France, when it needed things doing to it. Maintenance, things like that."

"So, you had no contact, other than through your solicitors?"

"No, not that I remember, that is." She shook her head uncertainly and seemed suddenly anxious to end the interview.

"Perhaps you heard of him through your children? You must see them sometimes, surely?"

"Yes of course, at Christmas and occasional birthdays. They used to tell me how Edward was and what he was up to, and I'm sure he heard about my life from them as well. But I must add, Inspector, that I have not told them of my illness and I would appreciate it if you would keep it quiet."

Bright nodded and she glanced at her watch.

"Good heavens! How time flies, Inspector. I don't want to seem rude but do you have many more questions? I have promised to meet some friends for luncheon. Nothing important of course, but I do hate to keep people waiting, and I am nowhere near ready. It will take me ages to do myself up fit to face them across the table."

"Nearly finished now, Mrs Ellis. Perhaps you could just tell me how you benefit under Sir Edward's will?"

"Of course, Inspector. I get the villa for my own and about eight thousand pounds a year to live on. That's the same as I have been receiving from Edward anyway. So you see, I am, in fact, rather worse off since he died as I now have to pay all my own maintenance bills and suchlike, whereas Edward paid them before. You know, eight thousand per annum for one's lifetime is not a great deal of money. Of course it was quite a handsome settlement ten years ago, but it takes no account of inflation. However, I shall manage. Edward's will does mean that I can sell the villa if I want to, and buy something smaller if I need the money, but I would prefer to leave that as long as possible. I love the villa, and it has so many memories."

"I'm sure. Well, that's all for the moment." He stood up. "Thank you for giving us so much of your time, Mrs Ellis. I hope you won't have to keep your friends waiting too long." He paused at the door. "I take it you won't be going to the funeral, then?"

Mrs Ellis had the grace to look slightly embarrassed at this question and rather hurriedly showed them out.

"I don't think I should intrude on Lady Ellis's grief," she explained. "I'm so sorry to have hurried you, Inspector. I do hope you can come to tea again and do bring dear Mr Dingwall with you," she said as she closed the door with relief.

* * *

The inquest was a very short affair, only taking evidence of identification before adjourning for two weeks. Bright spent the afternoon writing a report of his activities to date and sifting through the mass of transcripts of interviews with the general public who admitted to having been in the area of St Bede's that Monday night. These included fifteen separate reports of little old ladies in the area at the right time, and from the descriptions they were fifteen different old ladies! Bright sighed and made a note for those fifteen witnesses to be re-interviewed the next day – perhaps he would give that job to Hoppy. He needed someone who had the experience to sort out the facts and the hospital end of the enquiry was slackening off. He looked at his watch; it was nearly five o'clock. He decided to go back to St Bede's and tackle Nurse Jensen again. His job was to separate the wheat from the chaff, and Nurse Jensen, Bright felt sure, only rated as chaff in this case.

At the nurses' home reception desk Bright spotted one reporter attempting the frontal assault but he was unable to get past the receptionist. Bright wondered how many more were trying to sneak in the back way.

Nurse Jensen looked as sulky and miserable as ever and still wore the rumpled dressing gown with grubby-looking slippers on her feet. She greeted him in her usual friendly manner.

"What do you want?" she asked. "I've told you all I know. You've no right to keep pestering me like this."

Bright held up a hand in an attempt to stop her steady whine. "I don't want to ask any more questions," he assured her. "I just want to tell you a little story and all you have to do is tell me if it's true or not. Now that's not so very terrible, is it?"

"No, I suppose not," she said with a slight shrug of her shoulders. She opened the door a little wider so that he could enter the room. She sat down on the bed and watched while Bright once more moved her clothes from the chair so that he too could sit down.

"I'll tell you what I think happened about that drip. I think that you didn't change it before going to the cloakroom." He once more raised his hand as she began to protest. "No, let me finish. Not only do I think that, but I'll tell you something else too." He jabbed a finger in her general direction. "You didn't change it when you returned to the ward either, at least not for a long while."

He looked at her but she said nothing. She just sat there staring at him, her mouth slightly open and a frightened look in her eyes, so he hurried on.

"I think that you completely forgot about changing the bag until sometime later and, when you did remember, you went to change it and found Sir Edward dead. You panicked, thinking that you might have killed him, changed the bag, said nothing and waited for Nurse Banks to find him and raise the alarm. When the post-mortem revealed what you thought to be a confirmation of your worst fears, it was far too late to tell the truth. You decided to lie about when you changed the bag so that no blame could possibly be placed on you. It didn't matter. It didn't matter how many other people's lives you ruined or who might eventually take the rap for your actions, just so long as it wasn't you."

He was struggling to overcome the disgust that he felt for this mean and cowardly girl who had been such a hypocrite that she had accused Dr Cawthorne of the exact crime which she had committed, deliberately hurting others in an attempt to save herself.

"I don't know why I should be kind to you, but I will be," he said crossly. "Sir Edward Ellis had far more air in his veins than could have entered through a drip that had run through. There is no way you could have been responsible for his death through your negligence. Now that I have relieved you of your guilt, do you admit that what I've said is substantially true?"

"I don't believe you," she said stubbornly. "You are just trying to trap me into saying something incriminating. Well, I won't admit to anything."

"I'm not trying to trap you into admitting anything, you stupid girl," Bright said in exasperation. "Believe me, this was murder. Not negligence or incompetence, but murder. So, unless you went in there and deliberately injected air into Sir Edward's veins, that lets you out. So stop pissing me about and tell me what really happened."

"Are you quite sure I couldn't have killed him?" she asked in a querulous voice. "I mean, it's just that all this time I've thought it was me." She looked at him and he could see that she desperately wanted to believe all that he had said.

"I had a word with your ward sister and she assured me that only a small amount of well-distributed air could enter via the drip if it ran through, and Sir Edward got large amounts all at once. There is no trick, honest," he assured her, much more gently now that she seemed to accept his story.

The relief of discovering that she had not killed her patient must have been tremendous, but Bright was not expecting the sudden and intense change in Nurse Jensen. She put her head in her hands and great sobs seemed to wrack her entire body. He had absolutely no idea what he could do to stop the dreadful noise and just sat there, apprehensively waiting for the door to burst open and for hordes of irate nurses to appear and demand to know what he had done to upset her so badly. At last, she managed to regain a certain amount of control over herself.

"You're right. That is what happened. So, what do I do now?"

Bright sat back in the chair and rubbed his bearded chin.

"I'm afraid you are going to have to do another statement for us but, as far as the hospital goes, I couldn't care less whether or not you tell them what really happened. I'm not about to report you to the chief nurse or anyone." He sighed and added in an almost paternal voice, "Look, if you want my advice, I'd say that your best bet would be to tell Nurse Banks and the night sister, or perhaps your ward sister. I'm sure that they will understand and be able to advise you as to what you should do next. If you are lucky, they'll be able to keep quiet about it officially, and you won't be in any more trouble. We won't be charging you with making a false statement, just so long as you make a true one now. You will have to come down to the station to do it, but I can run you down there now, if you like."

She nodded dumbly, and brushed the tears away with her hand.

"Did you really see Dr Cawthorne go into the side ward at eleven thirty?" he asked casually.

"I may not have told the truth about some things, but I did about that," she maintained stubbornly.

Bright looked down on her messy and slightly greasy hair.

"What exactly did you see? And what were you doing at the time? It really is vital that I get the complete picture, you see," he explained, almost apologetically.

"I was just taking a bedpan into the sluice, to empty it, and fetch a few more bottles."

"Which door were you using?"

"The one from the corridor. The one straight from the ward creaks like mad, so we try not to use it at night," she explained, and then paused to collect her thoughts. "Anyway, I was going into the sluice and I noticed Dr Cawthorne coming through the door from the main corridor. I'm sure I wasn't mistaken because I could see him quite clearly in the light of the main corridor. I carried on into the sluice, looked at my watch and saw that it was only eleven thirty, so I still had plenty of time to go before my first break. I emptied the bedpan, rinsed it and left it on the floor next to the bedpan washer. We try not to use it during the night because of the noise and so we just stack the bedpans on the floor until morning. I saw that Mr Bryant had left a urine specimen to be measured. I did that and filled in the amount on the chart in the sluice, and I also filled in the time; it was twenty to twelve. I then went back into the corridor just in time to see Dr Cawthorne coming out of the side room and leave the ward. It was that which made me remember the drip, so I ran and got it and went straight into the side ward, but Sir Edward was dead and, as you said, I panicked."

"You didn't try to resuscitate him at all? Not that it would have done much good," he added; there was no point in upsetting her again.

"No, I know I should have, but I was so frightened. I didn't actually see that he was dead until I'd changed the drip because the light was so dim. I just ran from the room and hid in the sluice for about five minutes."

"Do you think anyone saw you when you went to get the drip, and do you think anyone could have entered the side ward in the time it took you to fetch it?"

"I don't know where Julie was. I don't think she can have seen me, and anyway she would have said if she had. The new bag was on the desk so I only took a few seconds to fetch it. No one could possibly have entered the room between Dr Cawthorne and myself, and if I didn't kill Sir Edward, I'm sure you don't need three guesses to know who did."

Chapter 8

After the morning briefing, reluctant to start work, Bright sat at his desk, absentmindedly playing with an ancient and treasured toy that had originally been a free gift in a boys' comic. It was a piece of circular cardboard, threaded on string, and it spun round when the ends of the string were pulled, making a whirring noise as it spun.

"Do you have to play with that thing?" Hoppy asked irritably.

"It's therapeutic," Bright answered shortly, but stopped playing with it and put it back in a drawer. "God, I hate working on Saturdays," he said as he got up and looked out of the windows. "It's almost as bad as working on Sundays. Right, let's go through those reports first, Hoppy, and then we will have to decide what to do next. God knows what Dr Cawthorne and Nurse Banks are up to. You and I will have to tackle them to get them to tell us the truth, if only to clear the way for the real investigation. Someone is going to have to interview the fifteen witnesses who saw old ladies hanging round St Bede's as well." He turned to the desk.

"I would have expected the witnesses to have seen countless young men in white coats, or young nurses returning from nights out, but no, it seems that the hospital staff had all left and the only people about were old ladies. It really is extraordinary." He shook his head and picked up a pile of reports.

"Let's see what the 'wooden tops' have dug up for us," he said. Hoppy muttered under his breath at his use of a derogatory phrase for the uniformed branch of the police force.

They had both been sitting there, reading quietly for a while, when Bright began to pull at the hairs by the side of his mouth.

"I see that Mistress Caroline's flat was up for sale, and still is for that matter. I wonder where she was going to move to, or rather, where Sir Edward was going to move her. It might be that he was growing tired of the woman, but you would have thought that he would have changed his will in that case. They were obviously up to something, those two, and we're just going to have to find out what." He leant back in his chair and put his hands in his pockets. He looked puzzled as he felt something unusual and drew it out with his right hand. It was the travel agent's card that he had picked up from Sir Edward's study.

"She is on the move; he was thinking of travelling. I wonder just how far they were intending to go?" He put his feet up on the desk and tipped his chair back, leaning against the wall. He studied the ceiling thoughtfully and continued to pluck at the hairs of his beard before adding, "Were they intending to go together? What was the wording on that florist's card, Hoppy?" he asked, suddenly sitting forward and bringing the chair legs back to earth with a bang.

"Uh, what was it now? Something like, 'Hanging around…' No, that wasn't it. I've got it written down somewhere, I know I have." Hoppy flicked through his neatly compiled notebook, very different from his boss's mass of crumpled scraps. "Ah, here it is. 'Prolonging my stay here. Don't hang around in hospital, Caroline.' Odd, that," Hoppy commented. "You'd have thought she would have come back to England on hearing that he was unwell, not prolong her stay in America."

"Unless he was supposed to join her, Hoppy. Unless he was supposed to join her. Look, you visit the estate agents, the travel agents and Naseby, and find out as much as you can about what was happening to the flat and who was going where. I'll go and see what I can dig up at the hospital. Unless you'd like it the other way round?" he asked with a mischievous grin.

"No, that's all right, guv. I'd really rather keep away from the hospital. You go and chat up the nurses again and I'll try and get something out of the bunch you've given me." Saying which, he picked up his coat and left.

As Bright was about to follow, he remembered the witnesses that he had intended to get someone to interview.

"Bugger it. I'll have to see them myself now, unless anyone else is free," he said to Sergeant Harper, who was chalking up a list of who had been sent where, when and why on the blackboard. She glanced at her list.

"There's a couple of constables who are supposed to be staying here to help out, but I can manage without them," she said.

"Thanks," Bright said. They were nowhere to be seen, so he wandered, apparently aimlessly, until he reached the lavatory door and then suddenly flung it open. Inside, two temporary detective constables were smoking and having a brief chat.

"Aha!" cried Bright in a jubilant voice. "Aha! Nothing better to do than hang around, gossiping like a couple of old women, eh?" he asked sarcastically, and walked around them, rubbing his hands with glee. "Well, I've got news for you, my lads. This isn't a geriatric ward, this is a police station, though I must admit it can be confusing at times. So, if you are free, which I take it you are?" He paused very briefly and then continued without giving them time to answer. "So, if you are free, you can do a little job for me. It won't take you long. These fifteen witnesses on this list here said they saw an old lady around St Bede's on the night of the murder. You two can go and re-interview them and get new descriptions. We want to know if they really did see anyone and, if so, was she anything like any of the descriptions given by the other witnesses. I have here several photographs of little old ladies for you to show them and see which ones they pick out. Try and get them to be more precise about the time as well and if they saw anyone else. Off you go then, have fun," he said as he bustled them out of the lavatory.

"And have a report on Sergeant Harper's desk by this afternoon," he called after them, grinning maliciously. They had little chance of doing the interviews in that time, let alone writing up a report, but it would make them sweat a bit.

When he arrived at the hospital, Bright asked for Dr Cawthorne at the main gate but was told that he was not on duty that weekend and must be contacted at home. Bright had forgotten to bring Dr Cawthorne's address with him, but he managed to persuade the reluctant porter to tell him what it was, although he did have to wait while the porter telephoned Dr Cawthorne to check that it was all right. Bright arranged to see him later on, in the afternoon.

Meanwhile he decided to go and visit Julie Banks and started to cut across the square towards the nurses' home. The sun was shining through the new leaves of the lime trees and it reflected off the moving spray of the fountain. The square was a pleasant and restful haven, cut off from the outside world on all sides by the hospital buildings themselves. Bright was just smiling to himself, thinking that spring had at last arrived, when he became aware of somebody smiling back and coming over to speak to him. She walked with a bounce that set everything jiggling, and although she was wearing a fairly conventional dress covered by a white coat, there was no mistaking the rather muscular bulk of Fiona Warfield.

"You're looking very pleased with yourself. I take it that things are going well, or shouldn't I mention it?" she asked with a cheerful grin.

Bright wrenched his eyes away from her admirable assets, which seemed to have got the problem of perpetual motion licked, and managed to answer, "As a matter of fact, I was only looking so cheerful because it looks as though winter is on the way out and it's such a lovely morning. I'm really looking forward to summer. You're being a bit keen, working on a Saturday, aren't you?"

"I'm doing a locum, actually. I need the money rather badly."

"I thought you were still a student?"

"I am, but because I'm well into my final year I'm allowed to do locum jobs," she explained. "I'm not allowed to do anything momentous like prescribe drugs, and pretty much everything I do has to be checked by a qualified doctor. Anyway, the senior nurses keep an eye on me too and make sure that I don't do anything too drastic, and it really is very good experience. After all, if I pass my exams, I'll be doing all this for real next year."

"If you're on duty, I don't suppose you would be able to get away later on for a drink? Purely a social drink, I can assure you," Bright asked on a sudden impulse.

"Oh, that shouldn't be a problem. It's a 'skins' locum, and the main advantage of that is the rarity of skin emergencies. I mean, acne and eczema are pretty awful conditions but not often life threatening," she said with a laugh. "As long as I stay within bleeping distance it will be fine, and I'd really like to go for a drink tonight, if you're sure?"

She seemed genuinely pleased and Bright wondered if it was the novelty of being asked out by a policeman. He hoped not. As he could not be sure what time he would be finished at work, he arranged that he would get the main gate porter to contact her when he was ready, and they went their separate ways.

Bright was still wondering what had prompted him to ask Fiona out when he rapped quite sharply at Nurse Banks's door, aware that she would probably be asleep at that time of the morning. He was taken by surprise when the door opened immediately and he was face to face with a rather tired Nurse Banks dressed in a sweatshirt and jeans.

"I wasn't expecting you to be up so late," Bright said by way of an explanation for his startled expression.

"I finished nights this morning and I'm trying to stay up all day to get back into a normal sleeping pattern. I'm not sure that I'll succeed, though," she admitted with a slight smile.

"It can be hell trying to readjust," agreed Bright, remembering his own time on shift work. He used to try to stay awake all day, drinking plenty of coffee, and then always had to get up several times in the night to answer nature's calls.

He came into her room and sat down in the chair without being asked.

"Did you see Nurse Jensen at all last night?" he asked, hoping to catch her off balance. She paused in the act of sitting down and then hurriedly settled herself on the bed, trying not to look confused.

"No, no, she's gone sick for the rest of her nights. Apparently it's all been too much strain and she's gone back home to her parents' for a few days' rest. I can't say that I blame her. If mine weren't abroad at the moment, I'd have been tempted."

"It's probably for the best, but it does mean that you won't know that she changed her statement last night. Most of it is not important to you, but you see we can definitely place Dr Cawthorne on the ward at about the relevant time. Now, did you see him at all between half past eleven and twenty to twelve that night?"

"No," she said uncertainly. "And Shirley must be mistaken if she says he was there."

"You're sure?" pressed Bright.

"Quite sure," she said more firmly this time.

"So he must have stayed in Sir Edward's room for the whole of his visit," Bright said thoughtfully.

"Oh," she exclaimed, and seemed suddenly unsure what to say. Bright just sat there in silence, hoping that she would decide to talk. The silence continued as he waited for her to say something, anything, to fill the void. Not saying anything can often be a powerful technique of interrogation and Nurse Banks was certainly flustered by it.

"Oh dear," she said. "I don't know what to say. He wasn't… I mean, he couldn't have. Why do you believe Shirley and not Dr Cawthorne and me? It's two to one."

"We have other evidence," he answered mysteriously.

"Oh dear," was all she replied.

"Right." Bright stood up. "I'd best get over to see Dr Cawthorne and see how he intends to explain it all away."

"Oh, you must give me time to think." She ran her hands through her hair in an agitated manner and then decided to tell him, "It was about half past when Charles came back on the ward. We had to talk something over. Something personal. He was very busy on Cavell Ward but reckoned he could spare me about five minutes," she said bitterly. "I saw him come into the ward. I was at the nurses' desk and we went up to the end of the ward, where there is a table. The patients have their meals there if they are well enough to get up. We sat at the table talking for nearly a quarter of an hour. Charles's bleep went off once and he didn't answer it, but then it went off again and he knew he was going to have to leave. I went with him to the nurses' station and he answered the bleep from there. It was Cavell Ward that wanted him, and he went there. Nurse Jensen wasn't anywhere around. Once Charles had left, I walked round the ward; I suppose I took a couple of minutes to compose myself, and then went into the sluice. Shirley was in there. We had a couple of bedridden patients who needed to be turned onto their other sides before she could go for her break. In fact, we took rather a long time doing them and she was just collecting her bag when I nipped in to check Sir Edward and found him dead. So she didn't get to her break even then." She paused and smiled slightly. "But that's the way it goes."

"Why didn't you and Dr Cawthorne say this earlier? I mean, there's no law against the two of you having a chat, is there?" he asked her in an almost fatherly tone. Nurse Banks seemed to have lost all her fight.

"It's a bit difficult and rather embarrassing. You see, Charles is married and his wife is very jealous. We have been having an affair and I had to talk to him because I think I may be pregnant." She began to cry quietly. "He says I've got to have an abortion, but I don't want to. He says he will deny it's his and that it would be blackmail if I threaten to tell his wife or anyone, and anyway no one will believe me. He says it would be easy for him to get half a dozen medical students to say they slept with me and that any one of them could be the father." The tears slowly ran down her cheeks and fell onto her lap.

"I don't want to kill my baby," she said desperately. "I want to have it. It's just that I'm so frightened. I mean, it would be all right being an unmarried mum for a week or so, but what about for life?"

Bright sat down beside her and put his arm around her shoulders, silently cursing Charles Cawthorne for putting so much pressure on such a naive child. She seemed to do whatever he told her, and Bright wondered if it was generally the case that doctors had such power over the nurses. He gave Nurse Banks his cleanest hankie and she blew her nose.

"I'll be all right now," she said firmly. "I shouldn't really have told you all that. It can't be of any use to you, but I do feel better for having told someone. I don't know what I'm going to tell my parents."

"That's always a tough one. Still, they'll probably take it better than you expect."

"I doubt it. You mustn't be too hard on Charles, you know; he's too weak, much too weak to do anything like commit murder," she said with rare insight.

"You know, someone else said that about some of the other suspects. I can't remember who it was, but this whole case is riddled with weak characters." He smiled and returned gently to his questioning. "Did you notice if Nurse Jensen seemed upset at all when you found her in the sluice."

"I'm not sure," she said uncertainly. "I was rather upset myself, but now that you mention it, she was very anxious to go for her break. She said she was dying for a cigarette and I'm afraid I told her rather sharply that she would have to wait."

"And how full was the drip bag when you went in to Sir Edward and found him dead?"

"I don't think I noticed. No, hang on. When the crash team arrived, I put up a unit of sodium bicarbonate and it wouldn't run through. I remember noticing then that the drip hadn't really gone through at all. I thought it must have tissued." She looked up. "That's quite important, isn't it?"

"Not as much as you would think, actually. It just confirms Nurse Jensen's statement." He looked down at the scrap of paper on which he had been making notes.

"So, Dr Cawthorne entered the ward at eleven thirty, came straight to talk to you, and you were then with him until he left the ward at approximately a quarter to twelve, if not slightly later." He looked at her. "Is that correct?"

She nodded. "Yes, honestly. I swear he never once entered the side rooms."

"Okay then." Bright rose to leave. "You'll have to make a new statement, I'm afraid, and I'll have to check all the relevant times, with the nurse on Cavell Ward and with Dr Cawthorne, but I reckon we've got it all sorted out now. I just wish you had both been open at first; it would have saved a lot of time and probably would have saved you a lot of anxiety. Take care of yourself." Nurse Banks showed him out, looking sad but relieved to have talked about her problems.

Bright finally arrived back at his office about four o'clock that afternoon. Dr Cawthorne had reluctantly agreed that Nurse Banks's new statement of the evening's events was substantially correct. However, he had taken great pains to make himself out to be much nicer. He maintained that it was doubtful that he was the father of the child, and that he had merely been giving Nurse Banks a counselling session on the ward. He had not mentioned any of it because he naturally did not want her embarrassed. He said that there was no question of his pressurising her into an abortion, although it was obviously the only sensible course of action.

Nurse Johnson, from Cavell Ward, had managed to confirm, when she had finally been located, that she had tried to get hold of Dr Cawthorne soon after eleven thirty and that he had taken some time to answer. She had been rather anxious about her patient's condition and distinctly remembered that Dr Cawthorne had telephoned back just after eleven forty-five. He had arrived on the ward a short time later and stayed there until his crash bleep went off. Bright had learnt from her as well that the crash bleep signalled the collapse of a patient and was different from and more strident than the normal one, as it summoned the crash team to the dead or dying patient. The bleep register roughly confirmed the times that Dr Cawthorne was called and the times of his responses, but the administrator did warn Bright that the switchboard operators were known to forget to fill it in at the time and then make it up afterwards, so it was not to be relied upon.

Bright sat down at his desk and put his mug of tea down amid the stains and rings left by dozens of others. A bulky report from the Fraud Squad had been left for him to read. He picked it up and ploughed through the first few pages, understanding little and learning nothing, before he gave up and just flipped through the rest. At the back he found a summary of the report and cursed the person who had made him waste his time reading the first bit.

"Any sensible person would have put the summary at the front," he muttered to himself.

The summary succinctly explained just what was thought to have happened. Sir Edward had been appointed engineering consultant with a committee of businessmen "experts" whom the government had asked to look into various rapid building methods and to report on which was the best and cheapest with regard to several government projects. The entire panel had come out in favour of one particular method that was only practised by one particular firm. This firm had subsequently got the contracts and built several buildings and the odd housing estate, which later had to be demolished as unsafe.

To be fair, Bright thought to himself, *they did stand for over ten years, which was longer than many people had expected.*

The Fraud Squad were at present investigating the possibility that the businessmen experts had been helped in their decision-making by the transfer of funds, and by other items such as expensive holidays and cars. Certainly, several of them had bought fairly costly items at that time, but tracing the source of the funds was proving very difficult. These men were all adept at covering their tracks to confuse the Inland Revenue, and the Fraud Squad were having considerable difficulty in uncovering them. They had managed to show that the then prime minister had stayed at one businessman's luxury house on a West Indian island and, indeed, that the money that bought this house seemed to have come from nowhere. The Inland Revenue were very interested in the house, and also in various sums of money that some of the others had been unable to explain away and on which tax had not been paid.

There was, however, no evidence to link the building firm with any of the committee, and this was where the

Fraud Squad had reached a stalemate. Until, that is, they had found a way of putting pressure on one member of the panel: Sir Edward Ellis. It seemed that they had discovered another little fraudulent sideline of that great man.

Sir Edward had been on several committees, deciding what contracts should be given to which contractors. While it could not be proved that he had been bribed into making these decisions, it could be proved that he had leaked the information to his son, Richard, before it was officially announced who was going to get which contract. Richard had then, under the cover of his firm, bought shares in these companies for clients who, when traced back through various different holding companies, turned out to be Richard and Sir Edward themselves. Although this did not always work out, they had, over the years, made themselves a fair amount of money. The Fraud Squad had offered not to prosecute Sir Edward and Richard on that charge if Sir Edward agreed to give evidence against the other five members of the panel. That gave the other five a pretty good motive for murder, except for one thing: Sir Edward had refused. He had been quite adamant about it and had even been in contact with the committee members and assured them that he was not afraid of facing the charges against himself and Richard. He would certainly not act as an informer. The Fraud Squad and Sir Edward both knew that he would get a less severe sentence for the fraud with Richard, unless he was given immunity from prosecution in return for information on the committee, and they were unable to offer that to him.

Well, thought Bright, *there we have the connection with Richard, all right. So far, so good. I wonder if the Fraud Squad will be able to press the conspiracy charges against him now that Sir Edward is dead? The case was pretty circumstantial to begin with, and Richard might only be found guilty of professional misconduct or something equally minor. I should think he feels a lot happier with his father out of the way.*

Chapter 9

It was not long before Hoppy arrived back, having spent a tiring day chasing loose ends. He was muttering to himself as he fetched some tea for both himself and Bright.

"I've traipsed halfway round London today, guv, and I still didn't manage to track half these geezers down. I don't know why people seem to think they can disappear just because it's a weekend, and I've never understood why banks don't open on a Saturday."

"You ought to join one of the ones that does, Hoppy, but I've got enough to sub you till Monday, if you want," Bright generously suggested.

"Don't be cheeky," retorted Hoppy. "It's not for me. I was merely following up a lead that happened to take me to a bank."

Bright waited while Hoppy settled himself comfortably in a chair and took the weight off his tired feet.

"Okay, come on, tell Uncle Jamie all. I know that you're dying to tell me everything you've been up to," Bright teased him.

Hoppy put down his mug and picked up his notebook. "First stop was the estate agents. They were a much humbler establishment than you would have expected Sir

Edward to use. The bod in charge was quite excited to have had such a noted client."

"Prestigious client," Bright interrupted.

"What client?"

"Prestigious. That's the word you should use, not noted."

"Personally, I think it's a word that a poncy fart-arsed poseur would use and I certainly would not." He paused. "Perhaps if I might continue?"

"You always were a Philistine, Hoppy," Bright said good-naturedly and waved a hand for him to carry on.

"Anyway, where was I?" Hoppy glanced at his notes. "Oh yes. He kept on about Sir Edward and how he had been such a help to the great man and had even suggested a firm of solicitors to handle the legal side of things."

"You mean Naseby didn't handle it?" Bright interrupted again.

"I'm just getting to that, if you could only wait a moment. You know we'd get on much faster if you let me finish and then asked your questions."

"You know I can't control myself, Hoppy; it's the way you tell 'em."

"Hmph, well, as I was saying, apparently Sir Edward had mentioned that he would want someone to do the conveyancing and the estate agent suggested a local firm, who did indeed deal with it all. He did say that he thought it a bit odd that Sir Edward didn't have his own man to deal with such things, but then decided that he might have been doing something slightly underhand as far as his family was concerned and didn't want anyone to know."

"Sounds plausible."

"Yes. I then asked if Sir Edward had found anywhere to move to, but the estate agent said that he wasn't interested in buying a property, only selling."

"Perhaps he was giving Caroline the 'big E'?"

"Well, it seems that she quite often dealt with the estate agents, so she obviously knew what was happening and she was quite pleased when they found a prospective buyer. They were, in fact, in the process of exchanging contracts, but he wasn't sure if things would go on, under the changed circumstances."

"That will be up to Mistress Caroline."

"Quite. Anyway, I wandered down to the firm of solicitors who were handling it all. They confirmed everything and said that they were just waiting for Sir Edward to hand over the deeds before the deal could be completed. They were rather concerned about where the deeds might be and I suggested that Sir Edward's usual solicitors might know as solicitors sometimes keep them. I managed to ring Naseby at his home. I didn't bother trying his office; I hardly expected him to work on a Saturday. He was extremely surprised to hear that the flat was being sold. He knew nothing about it and was a bit put out that Sir Edward had obviously not 'trusted his discretion in the matter', as he put it. Apparently the deeds are in a safety deposit box at Sir Edward's bank. Naseby hasn't as yet opened the box, but has been in touch with Lady Ellis about it. He needs to have the deeds to settle things for a start. He and Lady Ellis are due to visit the bank late Monday afternoon after Sir Edward's funeral and I suggested that perhaps we could open the box today. I thought we could possibly take a squint at Sir Edward's account and statements at the same time. Naseby was very happy to agree to it all and felt sure that Lady Ellis would be glad to help us in any way. He said that I should fix things up with the bank first, and even gave me the name of the bloke I should contact. He obviously knew bloody well that I hadn't a snowball's chance in hell of finding a bank manager early on a Saturday afternoon. In the end I had to settle for us to go on Monday as well and the manager, Mr Sanders, will be happy to see us then." He paused while Bright shouted to a passing police constable to bring them some more tea.

"Must just go and point Percy at the porcelain," he added to Hoppy.

"If you didn't drink so much tea, you wouldn't need to go so often," Hoppy called after him but was unable to hear the reply because Bright had disappeared through a door marked "To let", some vandal having removed the *i* soon after the sign had been put up. Bright and the constable with the tea arrived back at the same time and Hoppy waited for Bright to sit down.

"Come on, come on! We haven't got all evening you know," Bright pressed him.

Hoppy sighed. There was nothing worse than the guv'nor in what he called "one of his bouncy moods".

"All right, all right. Next stop was the travel agents on the card. It took me a while to find the person who had dealt with Sir Edward. It seems that once again these weren't his usual people. He normally used a large West End travel bureau, but this rather seedy little place near Holborn had fixed up just the one trip for Sir Edward, for the day after tomorrow." Here Hoppy stopped and looked at Bright with a self-satisfied smile.

"Well, go on, go on. This is what you've been dying to tell me all afternoon. What was it?"

"He bought a one-way ticket to Rio de Janeiro," Hoppy told him jubilantly.

* * *

As he waited for Fiona Warfield at the main gate, Bright was still wondering what on earth he was doing. She was way out of his class and as a rule he only went out with small and fairly dim girls who pandered to his ego. He felt at home with them and didn't have to try hard to impress them. This evening, however, he was about to embark on a date with an Amazonian, upper-class intellectual. It was bound to be disastrous even if she did have a magnificent chest. He saw her coming from a long way off, with her distinctive bouncy walk and a large grin on her face. He realised at once what had attracted him; it was the uncomplicated way in which she viewed life and her as yet unfailing good humour.

She took him to a little pub in a side street close to the hospital. She was still wearing her doctor's white coat and he was amazed to see her hang it up on a coat rack beside several others and nod to four or five people propping up the bar, who all sported bleepers in their shirt pockets. It was obviously a popular haunt for on-duty doctors. Fiona fought her way through the crowds to a quieter spot round the back where, at last, they managed to find a couple of unoccupied stools.

"I must admit I'm a bit horrified to see all these doctors knocking back pints and lighting up fags left, right and centre," Bright commented as they settled themselves on the stools. "Somehow you imagine doctors to be strictly abstemious, or perhaps quietly taking nips of vodka from a medicine bottle if they must have something to keep them going."

"Yes, I think the problem is that doctors often only have a short time in which to relax between cases and there is no doubt that a pint and a fag do seem to help. Obviously the danger is that you might have a bit too much and lose your ability to make clear decisions. Personally, I only ever have one pint when I'm on duty and I haven't smoked since I worked on the arterial surgery ward. Watching people losing limbs and undergoing really frighteningly dangerous surgery just because they've buggered up their blood vessels by smoking really brings the stupidity of it home to you."

"I'm sure it does," Bright agreed and then asked tentatively, "You normally drink your beer by the pint, do you?"

"Yes. Does that offend you?" She had a twinkle in her eye as he thought for a moment before answering.

"If you had asked me did I think women should drink pints, I would have said 'no' without hesitation, but somehow you don't look in the least bit odd with a pint. It sort of suits you, you know, fits in with the overall picture."

"I don't know if that's a compliment or an insult," she laughed and Bright grinned back.

"I'm not so sure, myself."

He was amazed that they were talking with such ease. He had thought that the difference in their backgrounds would make it harder to keep up a conversation, but the reverse seemed to be true. Always before he had had little to say to the girls he took out; they only seemed to want to talk about things in which he had little or no interest. Like most of his friends, he seemed to end up going out in groups, so that the men could talk to the men and leave the women to chatter amongst themselves. At least he was able to swap dirty jokes with the other men even if they had nothing else in common. He realised now that there had to be something wrong with that system. After all, he got to know the blokes better than he ever did his girlfriends. He had the feeling with Fiona, though, that he might well end up swapping dirty jokes with her and that she would know far more than he did.

As they sat, happily talking, a bleep went off, close to Bright's ear. The doctor who was being summoned quickly put down his drink and went out to the public telephone in the hall.

"God, those things make a terrible noise," Bright complained as he stuck a finger in his ear to stop it ringing.

"Not half as bad as the din the lady on the switchboard makes when she rings back the ward to put the doctor through. She tries to encourage the nurses to answer the phone as quickly as possible, probably because she is anxious to get back to her knitting. Anyway, she just puts her finger on the bell and the ward is plagued by a continuous ring until they can get to the phone to answer it."

"It must be diabolical on the ward with that happening every time anyone wants to ring them. How on earth do the patients manage to get any rest?"

"Oh, most of the calls are internal and don't go through the switchboard at all, so they just make a normal ringing noise."

Bright put down his straight glass of beer and started playing with his beard. "So you mean that you can tell whether a call is basically internal or external by the different sort of ring?"

"That's right. Of course, if you are answering a bleep from anywhere, you sound like an external call because you don't know who is doing the bleeping and have to go via the switchboard."

There was a short silence while Fiona watched Bright closely and he in turn gazed vacantly into space, still plucking at his beard.

"Is it the same at night," he asked. "I mean, you would have thought that there was some other way of attracting the nurses' attention, preferably without waking up the entire ward."

"There is. Once the nurses have finished settling everyone down, they switch off the bell and a dark blue light over their desk flashes instead. They obviously don't switch over until things have quietened down because they might not notice the light if they are busy." She had answered him fully but he noticed that the friendliness had gone from her voice and he gave her a quick smile of apology.

"I'm sorry. It can't be very flattering when I take you out for a social drink and end up pumping you for information."

"No, honestly, I shouldn't be silly about it. With my job, as much as yours, we are never really off duty. When you are in the middle of an interesting case you can't help but think about it, or talk about it, and anything that anyone says seems to bring you back to it. You just can't get it out of your mind."

Bright gave her hand a little squeeze and said, "You know, it's the first time I've ever been out with a girl who has had the remotest idea of what it is like to be in the middle of a case. I suppose I ought to have been more sensitive and not asked you out until after it is all over, especially as you know some of the people involved."

She grinned again. "Don't talk such rot. I'm a big girl now, I can take it. Besides, rumour has it that David's no longer a suspect, and I don't really know any of the others."

"You've got a very efficient grapevine," he said in surprise. "I suppose it's a bit like in a police station, no one can keep a secret for longer than five minutes. I'll have to watch out for you pumping me for information, as well."

"Oh, absolutely. Even the walls have ears," she said and they both laughed.

A little later, Fiona said she really ought to go up to the ward and check that there were no problems with her patients, and Bright regretfully walked her back to the hospital. He stopped to say goodbye to her at the main gate.

"So, how can I get in touch with you, always supposing you want to see me again?" he asked, uncertain what her answer would be and anxious not to be rejected.

"If I'm not on the bleep, you can ring the medical college and they will buzz my room, or you can leave a message with Bruno if I'm not in. And, yes, I would like to see you again if you think you can stand it." And she was gone with a smile and a quick wave. Bright stood there for a minute looking after her, then stuck both hands in his pockets and walked off, whistling tunelessly to himself. He stopped at the fountain and stared at the goldfish, asking himself why he had spent the evening with a girl whose main attraction had been her body but it had never occurred to him to try and touch it. He mentally kicked himself and went over to the nurses' home.

It took considerable time and a fair amount of effort to discover that Julie Banks was down in the basement social club. Bright finally found his way down there but was stopped at the door and asked for his membership card. The bouncer was unimpressed when he explained that he was a police officer on duty. Bright suspected that he had probably heard that story from half the Metropolitan Police while trying to fraternise with the nurses. Eventually, Julie Banks was located and she came and signed him in as a guest.

The club turned out to be a place of dim lights and many fruit machines, sparsely populated by off-duty nurses and on-duty porters. Disgusted by the range of pressurised beers and lagers, Bright bought himself a coke and Julie and her friends each something rather stronger. He noticed that they had all been drinking soft drinks until he offered to pay, and there was little chance of him being able to claim it on expenses. He sat down at their table and cursed as a helpful porter put some money in the juke box, making it impossible to hear a word that was said to him.

"I'm sorry to keep pestering you, but I just wanted to ask you a quick question," Bright bellowed, sure that no one could possibly hear him, but Julie was obviously adept at lip reading because she nodded.

"That's okay, fire away." At least, that was what Bright thought she said.

"I want you to think back very carefully to that night on the ward. I know that you have already confirmed that Lady Ellis rang, but I want you to imagine that you are checking the drip bag. Someone is calling out and you're feeling fraught."

The music came to a stop and Bright was able to continue in a normal voice, "All of a sudden the telephone starts to ring. You hadn't switched the bell off by that time, had you?"

"No, it was still quite early," she answered without hesitation, getting quite carried away.

"Right, well, as I said, all of a sudden the telephone starts to ring. Now, tell me about it."

"What do you mean?"

"Well, what was the ring like?"

"Ringing, like any other telephone," she said impatiently and gave him a look that suggested that she thought he needed his head examined.

"You're sure it was a ring-ring, pause, ring-ring?"

"Yes," she said, obviously worried and not sure what answer he wanted.

"It wasn't an impatient buzz from switchboard?"

"Oh, I see what you mean," she said with relief and looked thoughtful for a moment, closing her eyes to imagine the scene better. "It was a normal telephone ring-ring noise."

"You're quite certain?"

"Absolutely." She smiled at him, happy to have been of some help and blissfully unaware of the importance of her information.

"Thanks a lot, you've been a great help," Bright said as he left them and the music started up again. He walked thoughtfully through the crisp night air to the place where he had left his car.

* * *

"Right, lads, you all know what you're doing now, so off you go and do it," Bright said, finishing the Sunday-morning briefing. There was a general scraping of chairs and a certain amount of muttering and moaning as the day shift left the incident room and went to face their day's work.

"A word in your shell-like, Sergeant Harper," he called and waited as she came across the room to where he and Hoppy were standing. "I'd like you to organise a reconstruction. We'll start it from ten o'clock tomorrow night. We'll need to get all the staff who were on duty that night at the hospital and get them to hang around. No, actually, we've little hope of getting that. Just make it all the staff on the same wing as Sir Edward, and all the doctors and senior staff. All the porters and that as well. Which reminds me, did the super have a word with that shop steward about the fingerprinting?"

"Yes, sir, and it seems to have done the trick. Denison thinks he'll be able to finish them off tomorrow."

"That's great. Back to the reconstruction. We'll need plenty of men to stop people in the streets around the hospital and to check on movement at strategic places in the building as well. We'll also have to have men at the nearest Tube stations, bus stops and taxi ranks, stopping and talking to drivers and passengers alike. It's going to take one hell of a lot of organising, not to mention manpower, so I want you to start sorting it out straight away. Is that okay?"

"Yes sir, I'll get on to it at once, but I'll need authorisation from the chief superintendent for all the extra men I will need to borrow."

"I'll see that you get it as soon as possible." He turned back to Hoppy and asked, "What's the matter with you, then?"

"Sunday is a day of rest – at least it bloody well ought to be."

"Oh, a policeman's lot is not a happy one!" Bright sang cheerfully.

"Give over, we've got work to do. I see you've called off the house-to-house. Did anything come of it?"

"Not a fantastic amount of use. There are two people near Margaret Swainson's flat and one near Mr Penfold's who I think we should see later today and interview again, but first I thought we might both visit the indomitable Lady Ellis."

"What, both of us?"

"I need your moral support, Hoppy," Bright explained. "She frightens the living daylights out of me, so I want someone bigger than me around, to hide behind," he admitted as he stopped to take a report from a woman police constable.

"You're too kind, sweetheart," Bright said in his best Humphrey Bogart impersonation, which even he would have admitted was not very good, but all he got in way of a reply was a cold look as she went out of the door.

"And you wonder why you're never successful with women," Hoppy teased. "Perhaps you need to update your chat-up lines."

Bright pulled a face and waved the report at Hoppy. "Guess what this is."

"I've no idea. Give me a clue."

"Someone else for us to visit today, and I just know that it will make your week. I've decided that we shall arrange to take afternoon tea with that sweet little old lady Mrs Ellis the first."

Hoppy groaned. "I really don't think I'm up to it, boss, I really don't. Dingwall told me all about it and I always feel so awkward with delicate china and refined manners."

"Well, if you come and give me moral support with Lady Ellis, I'll come and give you moral support with Mrs Ellis. I mean, that's only fair, isn't it? I tell you, Sir Edward certainly knew how to pick 'em. It makes me glad I haven't met Caroline Harris yet. God only knows what she's like."

"Why have we got to see Mrs Ellis, anyway?" Hoppy asked crossly.

"Because three different and independent witnesses in the vicinity of St Bede's between eleven o'clock and midnight last Monday have positively identified Mrs Ellis's photograph. Apparently, she walked down Cockrill Lane and turned into the side entrance by the nurses' home. Now, why do you think she forgot to tell us that, eh Hoppy?"

"Oh," he said in a resigned voice.

* * *

"So, you still insist that you made that telephone call from here, Lady Ellis?" Bright asked in his most polite but disbelieving tone.

"Of course," she replied firmly.

They were sitting in the drawing room and Hoppy was looking extremely uncomfortable. He gave the impression that the slightest untoward movement of his large bulk would knock half a dozen gilt-framed pictures to the floor. Bright thought it surprising that Lady Ellis, who could not be described as a small woman, should look so at home in the overcrowded room.

"In spite of the fact that the switchboard operator does not remember putting your call through and the nurse says that it was an internal call?"

"I'm quite sure, Inspector, that you cannot expect switchboard operators or overworked nurses to remember, in all certainty, routine happenings like telephone calls. There must have been several calls to the ward that night and plenty to the other wards too. How can they both be so sure? I, however, can say with absolute certainty that I did not make that telephone call from the hospital. It would have been most extraordinary if I had done so, and I would be bound to remember." She was firm and very sure of herself, and Bright had to admit that she had a point, especially as Nurse Jensen could not remember what sort of a ring it was, or even that the telephone had rung at all.

"One other thing, Lady Ellis," Bright continued, changing the subject. "I understand that after Sir Edward had died, the night sister rang you, as next of kin, to inform you of his death?"

"That is correct, yes."

"But you didn't mention it before when we asked for your account of the events of the night. Why was that?"

"Good heavens, it completely slipped my mind. I've no idea what time she rang or even what she said. A sort of shock, I should think. I had completely forgotten that call." She seemed genuinely surprised and she went to show them to the door.

In the hall there was a telephone.

"Is that the only phone in the house?" Bright asked innocently.

"No, no, I have one by my bed as well and there's another in the study," Lady Ellis replied to his disappointment.

"Well, that was a bit of a wash-out," Bright commented as they made their way to the hotel where they were to see their next appointment. "Perhaps we ought to have taken her in to the station and leant on her a bit, but I don't think it would work. We can only hope that Mrs Ellis is more easily flustered."

"I doubt if she will be," Hoppy responded gloomily.

* * *

"I've been looking forward to your little visit all afternoon, Inspector, and your Sergeant Hopwood, of course. I know I shouldn't ask but I know that you must have some news for me." She fluttered around them, making sure they were comfortable and then dispensing tea. She seemed to have completely regained her composure since their last interview.

"No, Mrs Ellis." Bright gave her a slight smile. "I think you have something to tell us."

"Oh really, Inspector?" Her voice lost some of its sweetness. "And just what is it that you think I can tell you?"

"What you were doing at St Bede's between eleven o'clock and midnight on the night of the murder." He watched Mrs Ellis closely as she vigorously stirred her tea and thought about what he had said. She did not seem very surprised by it, just faintly put out that he had been so rude as to say it.

"I should never have tried to keep it quiet, Inspector. I never really expected to get away with it. I'm sure that if I were to call a solicitor, he would advise me to say nothing, but yes, I was at St Bede's about that time." She paused long enough for Hoppy to write everything down in his notebook. "After the taxi dropped me at the hotel, I went in and noticed that there was no one at the desk. I was agitated and wanted advice about something and decided to go and ask Edward for his help at once. I started to walk towards the Underground station, looking for a taxi as I went. As usual, there wasn't one to be seen, and I arrived at the Tube station a minute or so before eleven. Fortunately enough a train arrived almost at once. It is only a short walk from the station to St Bede's and I believe I arrived there at about a quarter past eleven." Having decided to tell Bright, she seemed anxious to be as precise as she could.

"I remember that, as I entered a small gate, a nearby church clock chimed just the once; I presume that indicates the quarter. I did not look at my watch so I cannot be certain. I hadn't visited Edward since he had been taken ill, and had no idea which ward I should go to, or indeed which part of the hospital. Somehow I had imagined well-lit reception areas and plenty of helpful staff, ready to point me in the right direction. Instead I found myself in a dark square with virtually no sign of life anywhere around. I thought that I must have missed the main gate and that it would be a good idea to try to find it. I wandered around for a few minutes, but I'm afraid I got a little lost and ended up at the other side of the hospital. I tried again and found myself at a gate opening back out onto the road from which I had originally arrived. I realised then that I was being a bit rash in trying to see Edward at that time of night. He would be asleep and the nurses were unlikely to let me disturb him. It was late, I was tired, and it had really started to rain with a vengeance, so I walked back to the station and took the Tube back here. Unfortunately, I didn't manage to get a direct train, but had to change at Holborn. There I had a considerable wait and it was quite late when I arrived back. There never is anyone at the desk after midnight – they just leave the keys out for the people who are in late. They must have assumed that I was already in my room, as I had forgotten to hand in my key."

She stopped and looked at Bright, waiting for him to ask his questions. She was far more intelligent than she pretended to be and she had proved that her memory was excellent.

"How long do you think you were in the hospital, wandering around?" he asked.

She hesitated a moment. "I can't say precisely, but I don't think it was much more than a quarter of an hour, probably less."

"Mrs Ellis, last time I interviewed you, you said that you had no idea that Sir Edward was ill, let alone in hospital. Tell me, just how did you know about it and, in particular, how did you know which hospital?"

To Bright's surprise, she laughed.

"You know, I was very silly to lie about that last time, Inspector, but I was flustered. It's quite simple really. It was in the evening newspaper, just a small paragraph of late news on the back page saying that Sir Edward Ellis was comfortable after an emergency operation at St Bede's. I don't know why I didn't admit to it before, except that if I didn't know Edward was in hospital, I couldn't really have been a suspect."

"I hadn't realised it was in the paper before his death. A bit of a slip-up on the information front there. Now, just one more question, Mrs Ellis. What did you want to discuss with Sir Edward?"

She hesitated for a moment, and then shook her head. "I'm sorry, Inspector, but that has nothing whatever to do with his murder and I have no intention of ever telling you about it. There is nothing more that I can tell you that will be of any help." She was polite but firm and no amount of persuasion would make her change her mind. Bright and Hoppy retired, defeated.

"We'll have to check up on Tube times and see if her story tallies, but she was there, Hoppy, she was there," said Bright. "She won't tell us why she was there, so it was obviously for nefarious reasons and she could have done it. I admit you do have to stretch the imagination a pretty long way, but she does have to be considered a possibility. I just wish I knew why else she would go there. You know, we'll end up having her down at the station too. Perhaps we ought to have the two old biddies down there together – you know, lock 'em both up in the same cell and eavesdrop on their conversation. Mind you, they'd probably kill each other before we found out anything. Come on, Hoppy, let's go and see those other witnesses that need re-interviewing."

* * *

The last of the day shift had long since gone to their beds and the night shift were leaving to talk to witnesses, or were busy typing information into the computer. Sergeant Reeve had taken over from Sergeant Harper and Hoppy had gone home to his wife, but Bright was sitting at his desk, a cold cup of tea at his elbow, a pile of reports in front of him and a thoughtful expression on his face.

He had always looked upon the gathering of the vast amounts of information that was so much a part of his job as a means of eliminating the innocent from his list of suspects. In this case, however, it seemed that the more facts and statements he collected, the more people appeared to have behaved suspiciously. It was true that two out of the three main areas of his investigation were less likely to be involved now, the hospital and the business committee having nothing to gain and a lot to lose if they were, but most of Sir Edward's family had lied about their movements on the night of his death.

Lady Ellis might have made her telephone call from within the hospital itself, Mrs Ellis had been there to see Sir Edward for God alone knew what reason, Richard had a less-than-satisfactory alibi, and now it seemed that Margaret had evicted her boyfriend as soon as they arrived back at her flat and could quite easily have reached the hospital in time to kill her stepfather.

One of the witnesses Bright had seen that evening was obviously suffering from an overactive imagination, but the other two were quite definitely telling the truth. One, a neighbour of Margaret's, had heard a man making a lot of noise at about eleven fifteen. He'd looked out of the window and seen someone whose description fitted Julian Penfold's admirably, knocking at Margaret's door and calling for her to open it. When he received no answer, he weaved off in a drunken manner and left the neighbourhood in comparative peace. The witness was fairly certain that shortly afterwards he'd heard a car start up and drive away, but he was unable to put a time to this and did not know if it was Margaret's car or not.

The second witness was even more sure of his facts. He was a neighbour of Julian Penfold's and the two of them knew each other well enough to go out for a pint every now and then. He had called to Julian as he passed at about eleven thirty that night. Julian had lurched his way up the steps to his front door before waving and calling goodnight, but he must have been too drunk to remember the incident. Even if he had walked briskly and in a straight line it would have taken him ten minutes to reach his own flat from Margaret's, so the very latest he could have left there was twenty past eleven, and in all probability he had left earlier. Bright had timed the drive from Margaret's flat to the hospital, and in the light traffic of that time of night and strictly sticking to speed limits it took him six and a half minutes.

Margaret Swainson quite definitely could have been there, and her bank statement showed that she was heavily in debt, which gave her a motive. She might not have inherited a great deal, but every little helps, and her mother was more likely to be a soft touch than her hard-headed stepfather.

Chapter 10

Bright shifted uncomfortably on the hard seat and flicked through the handful of leaflets and prayer books he had been given at the door. He always found funerals depressing, but when he attended them officially, they were even worse. They were always for people who had died suddenly, unexpectedly and often violently, and their relatives were still suffering from the shock.

Lady Ellis held on to Richard's arm as they walked down the aisle to the front pews. She was still dressed in unrelenting black, and clutching her capacious handbag; both she and Richard conducted themselves with great dignity throughout the lengthy service. David and Patty sat with Margaret in the pew behind and the three of them constantly fidgeted and whispered amongst themselves. The vicar gave a long and boring eulogy, dwelling on Sir Edward's illustrious career in the building trade. He talked of how Sir Edward had helped the world by building hospitals, houses and roads. Bright smiled as he thought of the Fraud Squad report which undoubtedly showed that he had helped no one but himself. He never knew quite why the police were expected to attend the funerals of the people whose deaths they were investigating. He had never learnt anything useful about a case while attending a funeral, and he invariably felt out of place. The theory seemed to be that the person responsible might be there, guilt shining forth, but it all seemed a bit unlikely to Bright.

Outside, he quickly buttoned his raincoat and turned up his collar against the all-penetrating rain and watched the family pile into a large black Bentley. The other mourners were also heading for their cars to join the procession behind the hearse to the cemetery.

"C'mon, Hoppy, let's go back to the station. There are one or two things I want to check before we meet Lady Ellis at the bank. Slim, you and Keller go on to the cemetery to watch the actual burial, and make sure that you collect all the cards sent with the flowers. Then, when the body has been decently put away, ask Miss Swainson to accompany you to the station. Naseby will probably come with her as well, as he's here. Just ask her to make a formal statement of her movements last Monday night and hint that we don't believe her – nothing too heavy – and then just let her sweat. I'll be back to interview her later." He turned and walked back towards his car, which was parked a little way along the street.

"I don't believe it," he said as he kicked the car. "I don't believe it, Hoppy. It's a Monday morning, a cold, wet and bloody miserable Monday morning, and some stupid bloody traffic warden has come along here and stuck a bloody stupid parking ticket on my car while I was at a bloody funeral. The bastard!" He kicked the car again, crumpled the ticket and chucked it in the gutter. Hoppy surreptitiously picked it up and put it in his pocket as he silently slid into the passenger seat. He would try to get it sorted on the quiet. Traffic division owed him a favour and Bright had been on official business, after all.

* * *

Bright had always found the large, old city banks exhilarating places. There was an aura of sanctity about them that was only comparable with ancient cathedrals.

But while reverence and adulation for an invisible god were totally incomprehensible to him, treating large amounts of money with respect had always seemed very right and proper.

They were ushered into an office by a soberly suited underling. The room smelled pleasantly of cigar smoke and proper polish and the whole office seemed to have a rather yellowed and dulled shine to it. Bright could image many generations of overweight businessmen and overworked cleaners all leaving their characters indelibly imprinted upon the paintwork and furniture, leaving the room with a paradoxical air.

Bright paused at the door to look at the assembled people. There was a florid-faced man standing behind a desk that dominated the room, tapping his fingers in a distracted fashion on the top of a safety deposit box. Lady Ellis was sitting in a sturdy chair by the side of the desk and merely looked up and nodded as Bright and Hoppy entered the room.

"Parking round here's a bit diabolical, isn't it?" Bright said by way of explanation for their late arrival.

"Perhaps you should do something about all the double yellow lines, then." The florid-faced man, whom Bright took to be the manager of the bank, Mr Sanders, seemed unimpressed.

"Shall we get on with the job then, gentlemen?" Lady Ellis asked. "I want to get back to my daughter as quickly as possible. I know Naseby is with her but I feel that I should be there too." She handed a key to Mr Sanders, which he took in a rather ceremonial manner and proceeded to open the box. Hoppy surreptitiously took out his notebook so that he could list the contents.

The box contained several bundles of stock certificates; Sir Edward's passport; a large amount of money in different currencies, the largest amount being in American dollars, the one truly international currency; an air ticket to Rio de Janeiro; and a large white envelope. Bright picked up the envelope and inspected it. There were no markings on the outside, but several stamps had been stuck in the top right-hand corner. There was enough postage paid for it to travel first class anywhere in the United Kingdom, but probably not enough to carry it abroad. He turned it over thoughtfully, slipped a finger under the flap and then paused fractionally to look at Lady Ellis and check that he had her permission to open the envelope. He tore across the top. Inside were several pages of typescript and Bright glanced quickly through them until he came to the last page. He read that one more thoroughly and began to fiddle with his beard. He felt everyone watching him closely as he went back to the beginning and spent a little longer looking at each page, pulling faces and repeating some words to himself. When he again reached the final page, he whistled quietly and handed them all over to Hoppy.

"It's a shame they are not signed and witnessed, so we can't use them as a statement, but I'm sure the Fraud Squad will be interested to know exactly what that committee were up to and just how they did it."

Mr Sanders cleared his throat and nodded towards Lady Ellis. Bright turned and saw her sitting rigidly upright in her chair and staring straight ahead.

"Do you have any idea what your husband was planning to do, Lady Ellis?" he asked gently.

"I'm sorry?"

She was too far away to have heard his question, so he repeated it.

"No," she replied shaking her head, unable to take in what was happening. She opened her bag, fished out a handkerchief and clutched it tightly in her hand. "But from the money, ticket and passport I would hazard a guess that he was prepared to bolt, if need be."

"It would appear so, yes, Lady Ellis. I'm afraid we shall want to take custody of all this for the moment. We will give you a receipt, of course." He looked at Hoppy, who started to make a copy of his list of contents, and then he turned to the manager.

"I'd like a statement of Sir Edward's personal account, covering as long a period as you can manage, if that's all right, Lady Ellis?" Bright looked to her for her approval and she gave him a curt nod.

"Yes, that will be all right. Perhaps you could see to that right away, Mr Sanders?"

The manager hesitated for a moment before saying in a quiet voice, "I feel I must advise you to talk to your solicitor before you agree to that request, Lady Ellis."

"Thank you for your concern, Mr Sanders, but my only interest is to find my husband's murderer because that way I will clear all suspicion from my family. No, if the police want details of Edward's bank account, then they must have them."

"Of course, I shall see to it at once," he said, and moved towards the door.

"Do you happen to know if he had accounts anywhere else?" Bright asked.

"No, he just kept the one personal account," Mr Sanders answered.

Lady Ellis continued, "He did have a couple of other minor accounts at different banks. He said it was for greater convenience." She gave a snort that was almost laughter. "They were meant to confuse the Inland Revenue of course. He wanted to make sure that his left hand didn't know what his right hand was spending. It is quite typical of him – he could be extraordinarily clever in so many ways. It is strange that in others he could be such a fool."

An embarrassed silence followed this speech and Bright was the first to speak, having decided to ignore all but the first sentence.

"Perhaps you could let me know where those accounts were?"

"I have no idea where they are, but I'm sure that Naseby does. I'll tell him to let you know."

Bright nodded and looked questioningly at Sanders, who was still looking rather put out that his client had patronised rival establishments, but he opened the door and spoke quietly to someone outside.

"The statement will be ready for you in just a few moments," he said.

"Thank you, Mr Sanders, and do you think we could possibly have some sort of box or bag to pack everything up in?"

For a few minutes they were kept busy listing, labelling and packing the contents of the safety deposit box in a case that was then locked securely. Lady Ellis was given the receipt, and she in turn handed it to Sanders.

"I think you ought to take care of this," she said. "I shall only lose it or something. If you will excuse me, I shall leave you all to it." She gathered up her bag and gloves and prepared to leave the room. Mr Sanders just managed to reach the door before her and open it. Turning at the door, she asked, "I trust that you will be returning to the station now, Inspector?"

"Yes, Lady Ellis. We'll see you down there, I expect."

She gave him a curt nod and left.

"Not a happy woman, that," commented Hoppy thoughtfully.

"You can hardly expect her to be," Bright said. "I know that she had few illusions as to his honesty in the business world, but it can't be all that nice to discover that he was going to play the rat on a personal level as well. I mean, there was only one ticket to Rio; he was hardly going to take the family with him, was he? As far as I know, he hadn't made any provision for any of them anywhere, either. If he were dead, it would be simple, but merely disappearing is a completely different kettle of fish; it might have taken years and enormous legal fees before any of them could touch a penny of the estate. I tell you, Hoppy, things get more interesting by the minute." He started to pluck thoughtfully at his beard, which was already thinning in patches, particularly at either side of his mouth.

"Interesting!" Hoppy snorted.

Back at the station, Hoppy was still complaining. "If you ask me, things get more complicated by the minute, not more interesting. I mean, take motives; so far, we can put anyone who benefited from the will on our list, not only to get their hands on the money but also to stop him disappearing and so end their present income. They would have to go through the courts to get so much as a shilling for the meter." He took a large swig of tea and continued, "And then we have everyone named in the confession, eight ultra-respectable business gents, and incidentally Richard yet again." He jabbed a finger in Bright's general direction, slopping tea on the desk. "If you ask me, things are looking pretty black for Richard. I mean, he's got stacks of motive, he has an alibi that stinks to high heaven and he's the one that looks the most like our friend the doctor – except for his hair, that is, but he still could have been mistaken for him. He has a similar build and perhaps he fluffed his hair up a bit or something."

Bright was busily mopping up the spilt tea with a distinctly grubby handkerchief. "You're not so keen on Margaret then?"

"No." Hoppy shook his head. "Okay, so she's changed her story now and admits that she chucked her lover boy out nice and early, but that's a long way from admitting to killing her stepfather. I mean she could so easily be telling the truth. She panicked because she didn't have an alibi and altered the facts slightly to give herself one."

"You're right, Hoppy, we can't just concentrate on her. It's about time we put the squeeze on Richard the oil slick and his alibi. We didn't find anything on his not-so-good lady, did we?"

Hoppy shook his head. "Not a thing, guv."

"That's a shame. We'll get Cummings on to it, get him to go round and question her again, then anyone who knows her, neighbours and that, and see if we can't track down her husband. We must find out if he's the jealous type and tell him all about his lovely wife. You know the idea – generally be as unpleasant as we can. Cummings is a smarmy little tyke so he shouldn't find it too difficult." He stood up and stretched. "With a bit of luck, she'll decide it's just not worth the hassle, or she might try and press Richard for more money, so we'd better keep a close watch on her. Tell Cummings to try and find out if she's been unusually flush of late, too." He tried to smother a yawn. "You'd better tell him not to go too far, though. I don't want him being done for pestering or anything, but he can push things as far as he thinks he dares."

"Okay, guv, I'll go and have a word."

As he got up, Bright made no effort to cover another yawn.

"Perhaps you ought to have a little nap as you seem to be getting too old to cope with the pace of life," Hoppy said and hastily retreated as a book hurtled in his general direction.

A WPC brought the book back and, in a very sarcastic tone of voice, said, "Yours, I believe, Inspector."

"Very clever of you, I'm sure," replied Bright. "Perhaps you should join the police force."

A temporary detective constable nearby snorted, rapidly took out a handkerchief and pretended to blow his nose.

Bright went back to studying Sir Edward's account of conspiracy and corruption and made a brief list of the people actually named as having broken the law. Apart from Richard Ellis, there were eight names and each would have to be investigated. They definitely had a motive to silence Sir Edward. *Especially if they suspected that the was about to run off and dump them right in it*, Bright thought.

He was puzzled by the account, though. It was not even a sworn statement. If Sir Edward had been planning to send it to the police, it would be useful to clear up a few points. It might even give them some new leads to work from, but it was not actually admissible as evidence. There was no proof in it; it merely stated what had happened from his point of view. Likewise, the newspapers would lay themselves wide open to charges of libel if they published it without proof. It did, after all, accuse several very important people of some rather underhand and definitely illegal activities. Unless, of course, Sir Edward had already given the proof to the papers, or had told them where to find it.

Bright stroked his moustache and went very carefully through the papers once again. There certainly did not seem to be any clues hidden there. So where was the proof? The fact that there had been no address on the envelope suggested that Sir Edward had not finally decided to whom he should send it. Perhaps he was waiting to see who was the highest bidder, but he could not possibly have told them all where to find the proof.

Bright winced as he pulled out another bristle from his beard and once again read through the statement. He was sure that it could tell him something, if only he could see what it was.

Perhaps Sir Edward wasn't going to be paid for it. Perhaps it was just an explanation, a way of setting the record straight, Bright thought as he looked at his list of names again and then feverishly searched for the original report from the Fraud Squad. He found it, eventually, underneath a week-old newspaper that he had never got around to reading and he quickly skipped through the summary at the end. Then he went through it more slowly, writing down each name as it appeared. Then he compared the two lists, one made up of names in the Fraud Squad report and the other of names in Sir Edward's confession. While the Fraud Squad list was the larger, it was interesting that Sir Edward's did have one name that they obviously had missed.

"Morris!" Bright called. "Go and see what info you can dig up on this geezer, will you?" He handed his chosen constable a scrap of paper on which he had written the name Thomas Lionel Woods. "I want to know about any connection he may have had with Sir Edward. And while you're about it, you can find out where he was on the night of the murder as well. Barry and Slim, you can tackle the others on this list," he said, and handed the two detective constables the rest of the names from Sir Edward's statement. "Treat them gently, now. They're probably pretty worried already, and I don't want to hear that any of them has had a coronary on their doorstep. Go on, piss off, you lot, and let your intrepid leader rest his feet and use his brain, which is after all why he is paid so much more than you plebs. Not that any of you have a brain to use even if they paid you to do so." He was more cheerful, almost euphoric now that he had found a new lead.

He glanced back at Sir Edward's papers and noted that Woods had not actually been on the committee but had been instrumental in bringing together various members of the committee and senior executives from the firm involved. He was the middle man, the one who had basically organised everything but, as far as the police were concerned, had managed to keep his nose clean.

Bright looked up as Hoppy manoeuvred himself carefully through the door carrying two mugs of tea, a packet of biscuits and a couple of files from which protruded several pieces of paper.

"What a man, what a star. Hoppy, my dear sergeant, you should be made a chief constable with your understanding of human psychology and the way you encourage your fellow men to work hard and with maximum efficiency."

Hoppy put everything down on the desk, pulled up a chair and sat down with a sigh. "I take it you've found something then?" he asked, and listened attentively as Bright explained about the extra man.

"What's in those files of yours?" Bright asked then as he brushed some biscuit crumbs from his shirt. "Shit!" he added as he noticed that he had dribbled tea on his favourite pale grey tie.

"Replies to assorted enquiries," Hoppy answered and handed Bright a moderately clean handkerchief with which to wipe his tie.

"Thanks," said Bright, dabbing at the stain ineffectually. "Let's go through them, then, shall we?"

"Right-ho." Hoppy put on his glasses and opened the top folder.

"Somebody answer that bloody phone for God's sake!" Bright snapped.

Once the ringing had stopped, Hoppy said, "Firstly, on the night of the murder, the last Tube from St Paul's should have left at eleven thirty, but in fact it was running nearly five minutes late. It did indeed stop at Holborn, but then that train always does, so Mrs Ellis could have known that anyway. No one positively identifies her anywhere along the line, although one girl did say that there had been an old lady in the same carriage as she was and it might have been Mrs Ellis, but she couldn't be sure."

Bright raised his eyes to heaven. "Dear God, why, oh why, don't people look around them? Why don't they open their eyes and notice things?" He threw Hoppy his handkerchief.

"To be honest with you, guv, if you asked me to identify someone in the same carriage as me a week ago, I wouldn't be able to, although I admit it would be nice if a witness could."

"God," Bright groaned. "Is it really a whole week since the murder? The chief will be doing his nut." He took another sip of tea, stood up and moved to the window. "Carry on, Hoppy."

"No taxi drivers, or bus conductors remember picking her up in the area, either, for what it's worth."

"Not a lot," Bright said pessimistically.

"Well, that's all in that folder. Let's have a look in the other, shall we?" Hoppy said bracingly, but only got a grimace from Bright in response. "Well, we have here a list as long as your arm of all the places that sell the type of syringe we're looking for." He handed Bright the piece of paper.

"Who's in my bad books at the moment?" Bright asked thoughtfully. "I should have saved Slim for this one; he might have lost a bit of weight going round all these places. Mind you, Fletcher skived off that bus depot job, so I'll get him to start his first thing tomorrow morning. He'll have to get in touch with everyone on this list and find out if anyone happens to have lost a syringe. Can you imagine the response to that question? Why doesn't he go and count the two million syringes in the stock room and see? He'll have to find out if any of them has any connection with our suspects as well, however remote."

"Right, I'm sure he will appreciate you thinking of him, guv." Hoppy laughed and went back to his folder. "In response to our attempt to get in touch with Caroline Harris, there's a message from the yanks asking if we know that she is booked to return to London tomorrow morning."

"Now that's mighty kind of the yanks to let us know. It might be kinda useful to talk to Miss Caroline Harris. I think it would be a good idea if we arranged a welcoming committee for her at the airport."

"I'll arrange that for you if you like, sir," Sergeant Harper said beside him.

"Thanks, that would be great. Have you got something for me?"

"Just the cards that came with the flowers at Sir Edward's funeral, sir. The girls have finished typing the details into the computer."

"Right, I'll have a quick look at them and then you can file them away." He put the cards on the desk in front of him and muttered aloud as he read them, one at a time. " 'Deepest sympathy', 'our condolences', 'from the Whitehead family', 'much love', 'great sorrow', blah, blah.

What does this one say? I can't read the writing." He chucked one over to Hoppy.

"I think it's some more condolences from someone called Terence."

"Oh, you could have fooled me." Bright read on, " 'Enid and the boys send their love.' Charles doesn't say anything. And this is dear Caroline's: 'Sorry you couldn't make it. It would have been great. All my love, Caroline.' Not exactly discreet, but doesn't exactly give the whole game away either. What else have we? More condolences and large amounts of sympathy from Uncle Tom Cobley and all. Well, well! What have we here?" He waved a small plain card under Hoppy's nose. "What was the name of the bloke I sent Morris to find out about?"

"Woods. Thomas Lionel," Hoppy promptly replied.

"Well, Thomas Woods has sent a bunch of flowers to Sir Edward's funeral."

"If you don't mind me saying so, guv, that's hardly anything to write home about. I mean, we knew they were acquainted and even did business together, so there is nothing extraordinary about him sending the flowers, is there?"

Bright was looking very smug as he leant back in his chair and stretched his legs out in front of himself.

"Not in sending the flowers, no, but the interesting bit is the wording on the card: 'For a brother-in-law I shall miss greatly, from Thomas Woods.' "

Chapter 11

It was another cold and wet night, much the same as when Sir Edward was murdered, and Bright surveyed the scene morosely.

There were uniformed police at all the entrances to the hospital, at bus stops, Tube stations and taxi ranks, and manning strategic points throughout the hospital. Six members of CID, excluding himself, were there to oversee the operation and Chief Superintendent Willard had promised to call in and see how it was going later. It was half past ten on a Monday night and all the chief characters in the drama, except the murderer and his victim, were ready to play their parts. It was time for the reconstruction to begin.

Bright nodded to Hoppy and walked briskly towards Hailey Ward and the scene of the crime.

It was eerie on the darkened ward with just one or two dim lights by the seriously ill patients and the harsher glare of the lamp on the nurses' desk. The two student nurses were standing by the desk with the night sister, uncertain what they should do next. The real work of the ward was being done by two other nurses, and their job was all the more difficult because the patients were all determined not to go to sleep.

"Right, let's get going then. Just try to do whatever you were doing last week. You will probably find it easier if you talk about what you are doing as you go along."

The nurses walked around the ward with Bright following and occasionally asking them questions. A little later Dr Cawthorne arrived, accompanied by Hoppy, and pretended to check the injection, and then give it to Sir Edward. The part of Sir Edward was played by a rubber doll apparently used by the student nurses for training purposes. In the dim light it looked horribly real with its half-open eyes and greasy skin. They all left the side ward, Dr Cawthorne left the ward, and Nurse Jensen wandered in and out of the sluice. The chief superintendent arrived to watch just before Dr Cawthorne came back and had his little chat with Nurse Banks. That finished, the doctor left, the body was discovered and the crash team came and pretended to resuscitate the doll. The whole reconstruction had gone very smoothly, but Bright had learnt nothing new. He wandered around the hospital for a while longer, hoping to find someone who had discovered something new, but he was disappointed. At one o'clock in the morning, he called off the reconstruction.

"That's it, lads, let's call it a day. Dingwall, you make sure that all the statements get back to the incident room. Sergeant Greaves is going to start putting them on the computer."

Chief Superintendent Willard came over and took Bright to one side. "Never mind, Jamie. We rarely get an immediate response from these amateur dramatics; perhaps something will turn up later. We've got to get this case closed quickly. I'm not trying to put pressure on you or interfere with your handling of the case, but you have got to solve it, and solve it fast. I'll see you in the morning." With a nod to Hoppy he left for his bed.

The rain had almost stopped as Bright walked slowly back to his car. "I can kiss promotion goodbye unless I find the murderer soon, Hoppy."

They walked in silence until they reached Hoppy's car.

"Something will have to break soon, guv, but it won't come any quicker for your fretting."

"Yeah. Okay, Hoppy, I'll try to keep that in mind. I'll see you in the morning too. G'night." And he walked off to his own car.

* * *

Next day, at the main gate, Bright asked the porter to bleep Dr Cawthorne and then he turned to Hoppy.

"There are more loose ends in this case than a plate of spaghetti, and much as we know that most of them have nothing whatever to do with the murder, we still have to waste time tying them up. There wouldn't be all these blessed loose ends if people didn't continuously lie to cover up their minor and often sordid little problems." He thrust his hands into his trouser pockets in frustration. "Mind you," he added, "some of 'em ain't so minor."

"Inspector Bright," the porter called to him. "Dr Cawthorne says can you go to Surgical Outpatients, please? He's nearly finished there and he'll see you as soon as possible."

Bright looked back as he and Hoppy set off towards the Outpatients Department and saw the porter laughing with his mates. "They're probably laying odds on whether or not Dr Cawthorne did it and when I will arrest him," he said.

"Apart from Margaret Swainson and her alibi, and Dr Cawthorne and his coat, what other loose ends are there?" Hoppy asked.

"Oh, Richard's lady, and there was David's lady, but we sorted that one out. Caroline Harris, the building committee's frauds, Nurse Jensen's fears, the syringe and the gloves, trips to Rio, confessions, Richard and Sir Edward's little scheme. I could carry on all night. Some of them are relevant, others aren't, but which are which?"

They arrived at Surgical Outpatients and had a word with the receptionist. She asked them to sit down and wait while she went in search of Dr Cawthorne. They sat in their allocated chairs and looked wearily around. The walls were covered in chipped and cracked paint in a shade of institutional green and spotted with posters of faraway places that the patients were unlikely ever to be fit enough to visit. Their old, worn and pain-filled eyes looked at Bright and Hoppy suspiciously from all directions, anxious that these two newcomers were going to jump the queue and make their already interminable wait even longer.

"They're still checking all the gloves for prints, aren't they?" Hoppy asked uncomfortably, more for something to say than from any real desire to know.

"It's going to be weeks before we know the results. Who would have thought that a hospital could use so many pairs of gloves in just a few days? So many different types and sizes, too. We haven't found any that don't belong, half of them don't have any distinguishable prints, and all those with prints don't have any that match those of our suspects. So now they have to be checked off against hospital staff, and there are still more than one thousand pairs that haven't even been looked at yet." Bright grimaced. "Can you imagine how boring it must be dusting several thousand gloves for prints and then checking them off? They must love me even more than the poor sods who had to sort the rubbish!"

Hoppy grinned. "Never mind, guv. It couldn't make you any less popular than you already are." He looked up as the receptionist returned and told them that Dr Cawthorne would be finished in a short while, if they did not mind waiting.

"God, how I hate these places." Hoppy complained, fiddling with the buttons on his overcoat. "I hope he doesn't keep us waiting long, or I shall start to get all morbid and overcome with painful memories of my prostate."

"Oh, bloody hell, Hoppy, anything but that," Bright groaned, picking up a magazine and flicking through it. "Why on earth would anyone want to know a hundred different things to do with an egg? And I can't see 'How the Pill affects your Sex Life' being of burning interest to most of the old codgers here. They probably think the Pill is for angina and a sex life is one lived by prostitutes." He got up as he spotted Dr Cawthorne as he came through one of the doors and beckoned them over.

"If you come this way, Inspector," the doctor said as they got to the door. "The consultant has already left, so we can use his room to talk." He seemed more embarrassed than concerned at seeing Bright again, probably because they knew so much about his private life. *Never do anything that you wouldn't want the world to know*, Bright thought to himself. *It's like wearing holey pants – you're bound to have an accident and end up in hospital.*

Dr Cawthorne ushered them into an austere room, decorated the same as the waiting room but containing a desk and chair, and a couch surrounded by screens in one corner. The only other piece of furniture was a battered trolley with a tray of notes on the bottom shelf and a lamp to display X-rays on the top. Dr Cawthorne sat on the desk and offered Bright the chair.

"No thanks. Hoppy, you have the chair. I'll perch on the couch." He climbed up on to his rather high seat and swung his legs.

"Will this take very long?" asked the doctor. "It's just that I've got to go to the ward and see a man who's not doing so well."

"No, Dr Cawthorne, it shouldn't. I just want you to think back to the night of the murder. You see, it's really important to find out what happened to that white coat of yours. It looks as though the murderer used it as a disguise and so we need to know where they found it. What I want you to do is to go over all your movements that night and try to remember whether or not you had your coat on, and if not, where it was."

"That's not as easy as it sounds. The trouble is," he explained, "I've become so used to wearing it that I don't really notice it anymore. You know, it's like most people and their suit jackets but probably even more difficult."

"I know, I know, Dr Cawthorne, but if you could just try to remember. It could be important."

"Well, I certainly had it on when I did my evening rounds, because I remember putting it on in my room before going on the wards. First, I went to Lister, and then Edith Cavell, where I got rather caught up, and it was a long while later before I went to Hailey. I know I had my coat on when I left there because I remember walking along and my ophthalmoscope falling out of the pocket. I discovered a hole in the pocket and I was livid because the ophthalmoscope was broken and they are bloody expensive things to replace, you know. I transferred everything to my jacket pocket, but I left the coat on while I nipped back to Cavell Ward."

"So you were wearing a jacket as well as the coat?" Bright asked.

"Yes, I often do at night. It can get very cold in the corridors and crossing the square," the doctor explained. "At half past eleven I went back to Hailey Ward and, come to think of it, I didn't have my coat on while I was talking to Julie. I know that because I can remember… Well, never mind that," he said hastily, and then continued, "Now, where did I take it off? I think I must have taken it off before going on the ward. Oh yes, I remember now, I left it on the chairs outside because I was, in fact, rather warm. Come to think of it, when I rushed back to Cavell, I didn't pick it up. I know I didn't have a coat on there because I got blood on my jacket, so I must have left it on those chairs outside Hailey," he finished jubilantly.

"That's really tremendous, Dr Cawthorne. Literally anyone entering Hailey Ward could have put on your white coat and pretended to be a doctor in order to murder Sir Edward," Bright said bitterly.

"Sorry about that, but you can't expect me to anticipate that sort of thing, can you?"

"I suppose not, Dr Cawthorne, I suppose not."

* * *

"So, Nurses Banks and Jensen both corroborate Dr Cawthorne's account of his white coat," Bright said. "I'm glad to hear that Nurse Jensen was suitably apologetic when she realised the significance of the fact that he had not been wearing a white coat on entering the ward but that whoever left the room later was wearing one. It's quite obvious now that while Jensen was in the sluice and Banks and lover boy were having their little heart to heart, someone slipped into Sir Edward's room wearing the white coat and it was him that Jensen saw leaving the room after he had done the dirty deed."

"You know, that Nurse Jensen is just terrible," said Hoppy, who had been given the task of questioning her while Bright had had the much easier job of seeing Nurse Banks.

"I know," agreed Bright. "She's so convinced that no one will like her because she's plain and dim that she doesn't notice that no one likes her because she's such a moaner."

"She's decided to leave nursing," Hoppy continued. "She's only back here to work out her notice. Just as well, I should say. I don't think she was suited to nursing."

"No, you're right there." Bright said. "Forensics confirmed that there was a hole in the coat's right-hand pocket, and just to make our day, Hoppy," he added, "fingerprints just phoned us to say that none of our suspects' prints were found on any of the gloves, but it will take them another month of Sundays to find out just whose prints are actually on them. I don't think we'll get anything there. Our murderer is a clever old sod and probably chucked the gloves away outside the hospital somewhere, like Land's End or John o' Groats. Or, he might have used one of the many pairs without clear prints on, anyway. No, we'll probably never know what happened to them."

"Well, just exactly where does that leave us, guv? I mean, you seem to know what you're up to, but I'm blessed if I know what's going on," Hoppy grumbled.

"It's elementary, my dear old Watson. All you've got to remember is that most of the facts have nothing whatever to do with the murder at all. Then you have to sift out the few totally unexplainable ones and treat them as bona fide clues. That way you should come to only one person. The only trouble is, I seem to have come to three if not four people, but I refuse to believe that they were all in it together. That would be a cop-out."

"Well, I'm glad to hear that you are so optimistic," Hoppy continued in his grumbling way. "Listen to that now," he said, pointing to the door. "I can hear the battle-axe telling someone we're still hard at work here and I was hoping to get home a bit earlier this evening."

Bright turned to the door just as Detective Constable Cummings entered with Richard's lady in tow.

"Oh, hello Cummings," he said cheerfully. "And hello Miss, or rather Mrs de Loro. Had a change of heart, have you? Remember a previous engagement that night? Huh?"

She just played with the rings on her fingers.

Cummings said, "I think Mrs de Loro would like to make a new statement, guv. It appears that Mr Ellis used untoward persuasion to force her into making her last statement."

"Oh yes? Used a bit of blackmail, did he? Or was it physical force, Mrs de Loro? Would you like to press charges?"

"No," she said quickly. "No, I just want to change my statement, if that's all right, but you must guarantee that you won't charge me with anything if I do change it. I don't want to get into any more trouble. Constable Cummings said you knew what had happened anyway and that Richard was really at home. He said that you were going to charge me with obstruction or something, but that if I changed my statement, you wouldn't."

Bright looked at Cummings and raised his eyebrows, but Cummings was staring solidly at his feet. "That's right, guv, isn't it?" he said to his big toe.

"Yes, yes, that's quite right," Bright quickly agreed.

"Right, well then, Richard wasn't with me at all that evening. I don't know where he was but he wasn't with me at any time. He asked me to say that he was and he used some information he had to make me do as he said. There was no money involved whatsoever," she said categorically.

"I'm sure there wasn't," Bright said soothingly. "Cummings, take Mrs de Loro to an interview room and take down her revised statement, will you?" He watched them leaving the room and added, "Oh, and Cummings? That was a good job."

Cummings smiled appreciatively. It was rare indeed for Bright to give praise and he was unlikely to forget this job, his first major crime investigation, for that alone.

"Right, well, I'll be off then," Hoppy said hopefully.

"What?" asked Bright. "What time is it then?" He looked at the clock above the door. "Jesus, Hoppy, it's only six o'clock, you can't go yet."

"Guv, that clock has said six o'clock for the past six months regardless of what time it is. The real time is half past nine, long past my supper time, and Gladys will be getting worried. Oh God, not another report," Hoppy said despairingly as he was handed another sheet of paper, which he passed straight over to Bright.

"Yes, Hoppy, another report. Hallelujah, another report, and it's a real goody. The reconstruction has come up trumps, look."

The computer printout that he showed to Hoppy stated that five witnesses interviewed at the back of the hospital during the reconstruction had also been there during the relevant times, one week earlier. Four of them remembered a red Renault Five parked illegally and with its side lights on, by the back entrance of the hospital. One remembered that it was a C registration and another thought there had been a no-smoking sticker on the side window. The computer also reported that Margaret Swainson owned a red Renault Five, registration number C159 AZO.

"Not bad, guv, not bad. I'll check the car out first thing in the morning on my way in for report. I'll just go home now, if you don't mind."

"Sure, Hoppy. Oh no, hang on one minute. Hello, Fletcher. Don't tell me you've come to report at this time of night? Hoppy will never get home."

"That's right, guv. I thought you'd like to know that I've got a lead on the syringes."

"Fantastic, this must be my lucky night," said Bright. "Let's be having it."

"The Ellises' family doctor used the type of syringe we're looking for. They keep them in a store cupboard outside the waiting room, where no one can see the door. It's only locked at night. They have no idea if any are missing and have no way of telling. You'll be pleased to hear that in the last six months, all the Ellises and Miss Swainson have seen the doctor, although I can't find out why any of them saw him."

"Great, Fletcher," Bright said despondently. "That's really great, but it doesn't exactly narrow down the list of suspects too much, does it?"

"Well, if that is finally all, I'm off to my burnt supper and long-suffering wife. What are you up to, guv?"

"I'm going to meet Fiona for a quick drink and see if I can twist her arm to join me for a curry."

"Yuk! I've never liked that stuff. Can't see what you see in it, but I hope you have a nice time. See you in the morning."

"Bye, Hoppy. Give my apologies to Gladys."

* * *

Bright lay in bed, staring at the patterns of light on the ceiling. They were made by a nearby street lamp and the flimsy curtains hardly blocked the light at all.

"I only seem to have talked to people," he said with a sigh.

"What?" she said sleepily.

"All I seem to have done is talk to people," he repeated.

Fiona pulled herself up into a sitting position, allowing the quilt to fall to her waist and reveal her breasts.

"Well, personally I'd say you did a little more than talk tonight," she teased.

"You know what I mean," he laughed and stroked her hair. "I've talked to people and I've summed up their characters. I've persuaded people to tell me lots of sordid little things about their private lives, things that really would have been better left in the dark, but I had to know just so that I could eliminate the irrelevant ones. But we seem to have very few solid facts. I have nothing that I can pick up and hold in my hand and say so and so must have done it because of this. We have motives, opportunities and lots of circumstantial evidence, but no damn proof. The forensic scientists haven't been able to come up with so much as a bit of fluff. Nothing but air in the syringe. No prints. All the suspects' clothes show that they have been in the hospital at some point, and none of them has an alibi. In fact, I know that most of them were in the hospital that night, possibly even when the murder was committed, but I can't prove that any of them did it. I have absolutely bugger all to show a jury."

There was a pause, as they both thought about it.

"What do you think Julie Banks will do with the baby?" he asked, changing the subject.

"I don't know for sure," she answered. "I think that she'll have it, and Cawthorne will have to stump up the maintenance. I just hope she screws him for every penny she can get."

"It's not just her though, is it?" Bright cut in angrily. "The poor kid will suffer too, won't he? I'm always dealing with people who won't take responsibility for their actions."

"Cawthorne believes that he is taking responsibility for his actions. He sees that he made a mistake and he would like best of all for Julie to go into a clinic overnight and rid them both of the problem. She won't do that, so he sees it essentially as her problem now. Having made the decision that the baby is best swept under the carpet, or up the hoover would be a more apt saying," she said bitterly, "he wants no further responsibility. The baby is dead in his eyes."

Bright shook his head, unable to understand. "If that's the way he feels, he ought to have the snip – you know, a vasectomy. If he is not prepared to care for his children, mistakes or otherwise, he ought to make bloody sure he doesn't have any."

"Oh, I agree with you. I was trying to explain his point of view to you, but in no way do I condone it. The man's a bum, but I'm surprised at your attitude. Most men would say it was Julie's fault for not taking adequate precautions. In this day and age of the Pill, men seem to regard contraception as solely the woman's responsibility."

"Maybe that's understandable if you're talking about women, but Julie is just a girl, probably still a teenager. Dr Cawthorne is older, he should have realised that. Anyway, this is rather a deep and meaningful conversation for the middle of the night, isn't it?" he asked as he gently stroked her bare shoulder and began nibbling at her ear.

“And just what is the correct conversational content for the middle of the night?” she said, trying to remain serious but giggling in spite of herself. “Don’t swallow my earring, I’ll never find another like it.”

So he kissed her instead.

Chapter 12

On the way to Richard's office, Hoppy briefed Bright on his visit to Margaret Swainson's flat. Hoppy had found the red Renault Five, registration C159 AZO, parked along the road, and he had inspected it without disturbing Margaret. On the near side-light window, there was a red, triangular no-smoking sticker.

"Looks almost certain that she was there, then, Hoppy," Bright said as he drove round, trying to find a parking space. He finally found one, quite a long way from his destination. "And it's sodding-well raining again," he muttered as they walked along the city streets to the large, modern office block where Richard's firm had its offices.

"I've never been in a stockbroker's office, Mr Ellis," Bright said as he wandered around, looking at the pictures, inspecting the furniture, opening the drawers. It was very plush with modern leather and tubular steel furnishings. The walls were covered with neutral hessian and very modern oil paintings in lurid colours. The vertical blinds were only half open so that the room had to be lit from a haphazard arrangement of glass stalactites suspended above the desk.

"Do sit down, Inspector. I'm sure you will be able to examine the room just as well from the chair."

"It will restrict me a little, but if you insist."

"Perhaps if you could tell me the reason for your visit I could deal with it and get back to work, Inspector. I am a very busy man, you know." Richard was trying to appear calm but he was nervously toying with a pen.

"Right then, Mr Ellis. Where were you on the night of the murder?"

"Really, Inspector, I have already made a statement as to my whereabouts on that night, as did Mrs de Loro." He smoothed his hair back from his forehead and then went back to fiddling with the pen. "I do feel that you would be more likely to catch my father's murderer if you go and search the streets with a magnifying glass rather than spending your time asking us mindlessly repetitive questions."

Desiree de Loro had obviously not thought fit to get in contact with Richard and tell him about her retraction. *He's in for a bit of a shock*, Bright thought to himself and smirked.

"Mrs de Loro changed her statement last night, Mr Ellis. I'm surprised she didn't get in touch with you to warn you about it. I do hope you haven't wasted too much money on her."

"I'm sure you must have made a mistake, Inspector. I was with Mrs de Loro that night. If you have forced her to change her statement by putting undue pressure on her, I shall complain to the chief constable. I am not without influence, you know." He paused, expecting some sort of response, but Bright remained stony-faced.

"It's true," Richard said indignantly. "I'm not."

Bright just sat and watched as Richard's confidence slipped visibly.

"I'm not, honestly I'm not," he added feebly.

As Bright continued to sit in silence, Richard soon stopped talking. He had a sulky expression on his face and he finally said, truculently, "All right, I was at home, alone all the evening and night. I was busy checking some figures that I needed for the next day. I can't prove it. I have no witnesses. I panicked when you asked us for alibis. It just seemed easier to invent one than admit the truth. After all, I knew I didn't have anything to do with the old man's death, so there didn't seem to be any harm in it. I thought it would help me avoid a lot of unnecessary suspicion and trouble."

"You ought to know better than that, young man," Bright said pompously. "You're supposed to be intelligent. You are a successful stockbroker. That takes brains, guts, initiative and a gambler's heart, so I believe, and somehow that description doesn't bring you to mind. How have you succeeded in this business? You did so only because of Daddy's help, didn't you?" He looked at Richard with disdain, a Richard who was so frightened and angry that he had gone very pale and shook slightly.

"How did you know we were working together?" he stammered.

"You must have known that the Fraud Squad had uncovered your little conspiracy," Bright said harshly. "They even came to you and told you that they were going to prosecute you unless your father testified against the building committee."

"Oh God, what a mess!" Richard said in a voice that broke slightly. "He used me as he always did, and when I got scared, because he was taking too many risks, he told me he'd tell the police that he had no idea that I was using information from him to make money." He looked at Bright in despair. "I begged him to let me stop and I begged him to testify against the building committee, but he wouldn't. He didn't care what would happen to me, he just thought that he could get away with it all. I'd be sent to prison and he would bluff it out. He would have sent me there, he would have, if I hadn't stopped him." He looked at Bright in silent appeal.

"Perhaps you wouldn't mind accompanying us down to the station, Mr Ellis," was all Bright said.

* * *

That afternoon they left Richard in the interview room with a constable who had strict instructions not to talk to him at all, and went to call on Caroline Harris at her Pimlico flat. It no longer seemed to be up for sale and although it had been empty for only a short time it had a musty, damp smell to it. The furniture, rather than being smart or expensive, was more comfortable and well-loved. Obviously, many things had been hers as a child and other pieces had been added from antiques' stalls and auctions. The chairs were high-backed, well-padded but tending to sag. They were covered in cushions of all shades and varieties. The pictures on the wall included framed prints and posters, and there were multi-coloured rugs on the floor. Despite having a slightly fussy effect, the flat was none the less cosy and cheerful.

Bright settled himself comfortably into an old, corduroy-covered armchair with worn patches on the arms and an anti-macassar over the back. He was taken aback by the blunt way in which Caroline started the conversation once they had all seated themselves.

"How much do you know?" she asked.

"How much do I know about what?" Bright countered.

She paused, hesitating only a few seconds before continuing, "I presume that you are aware of Teddy's involvement with the Fullerton building committee, and that you probably have a good idea about his dealings with Richard."

She looked at Bright, who nodded, and then carried on, "What I'm less certain about, is whether or not you know that Teddy was about to sell the story and elope with me to Rio." She paused for effect and was faintly irritated when Bright cut in.

"Yes, yes, we know all that. What we want to know, is who else knew what you were up to and who was buying the story off Sir Edward."

She was obviously thrown by his aggressive response. She had decided beforehand what she was going to say, and how, but the interview was not running to plan.

"As far as I know, the only other people in on the scheme were John Orson and his brother."

"The Right Honourable John Orson, MP?" Bright queried.

"That's right. You see, the deal was for Teddy to give his statement to John. Then, when he'd left the country, John would ask questions in Parliament on the subject, using the statement which could then be reported in full in the *Clarion*, the paper edited by his brother, without fear of a libel action."

"Oh, very neat," said Bright in admiration. "I hadn't thought of that particular loophole in the libel laws. If they trod carefully, I can see that the paper could cover itself pretty well. Rupert Orson must bless the day his brother became an MP, humble backbencher though he is. Mind you, it's probably a case of 'if I scratch your back, you scratch mine'. I suppose it was Rupert who was to pay Sir Edward for all this?"

"That's right, but he won't pay up now, even though John will probably still ask his questions. The thing is, the *Clarion* will be no better off than the other papers because they don't have Teddy's statement."

"It's a hard life, isn't it?" Bright commented in a mocking voice.

"Look, you may think I'm just another gold digger, but I'm not," she said hotly. "I genuinely cared for Teddy. Oh, I'm not saying that I was in love with him or that I would have considered running off with him if he wasn't loaded, but I would have given him a much better run for his money than the old hag he was already lumbered with. Oh, sorry," she added as her rather violent accompanying gestures dislodged an ashtray and scattered cigarette ends over Bright's trouser legs.

"That's all right," he said as he brushed them and instantly regretted it when his hand became grey with the ash. He distractedly wiped his hand on his handkerchief, while Caroline picked up the butts and replaced them in the ashtray. She then returned the ashtray to its former precarious position on the arm of her chair and lit another cigarette.

"Have you ever met Lady Ellis?" he asked tentatively, anxious not to provoke any more outbursts likely to dislodge the ashtray again.

"Just the once," Caroline said, "but Teddy talked about her a lot – and I know that it's likely he gave me a rather biased viewpoint, but it can't all have been lies. Some of it must have been true, especially the bits about putting on a show in public. No one must ever suspect that anything is wrong. According to Teddy, she said before they were even married that she didn't mind how many affairs he had because she wasn't interested in sex anyway. All she required was that he should conduct them discreetly. No one must ever know. I can imagine her being like that." She stopped talking and, as Bright and Hoppy left, she seemed lost in thought.

* * *

While Bright waited for the men to assemble for the evening briefing, he stood in his usual position, staring out of the window into the street below. He watched the workers scurrying home for their tea, all looking straight ahead, too intent on their own purposes to notice anyone or anything around them.

Bright felt depressed, as he always did in the final stages of this sort of investigation. At first there was the exhilaration of the hunt, pitting his wits against the murderers, not knowing who was going to win. With the average killer that stage lasted no time at all and then there was the arrest or a laborious and boring search for proof. Occasionally there was a case where the killer had used skill rather than brute force, subtlety rather than raw and all too apparent emotion, and then he had to hunt them like a gillie stalking a stag. It was then that Bright would begin to feel close to the killer, the hunter developing an attachment for his quarry. When he knew who they were, and knew that he had them cornered, then there was a feeling of deflation. He would have to bring them to trial, reel them in, make the kill. But he had not got this murderer cornered yet; he was very near but needed something more solid to close the case.

Actual proof he knew in his heart he would never have, the killer had been far too clever for that, but there had to be a weakness, a flaw in the plan big enough for Bright to get hold of and bring the case home. He stood there going over all the facts looking for this flaw, desperately searching for anything odd. He was pleased that at least all the members of the building committee had managed to produce reasonable alibis. They were another red herring and it was a great relief to write them off his suspect list. He was less pleased to have had to let Richard go. He had thought that Richard might be the toe-hold in the case, which he would work at and turn into cast-iron proof. Bright had given him a grilling and tried to put him under pressure but Richard had refused to say anything until his solicitor was present, and he had not needed to hold out for long. Richard's secretary had telephoned Naseby before Bright had left the building and, once he had arrived, the solicitor had wasted no time at all in pointing out that all the evidence was circumstantial. He had sprung Richard before Bright had managed to get anything out of him.

* * *

Margaret was firmly denying that her car had been parked outside the hospital on the night of the murder and it would be impossible to prove conclusively otherwise.

Bright was still standing, looking out of the window at the lines of headlights, when his telephone rang. It was the desk sergeant from Chelsea police station to say that the constable on duty outside the Ellis household had radioed in, requesting support.

"I thought you might like to know that Richard Ellis seems to have shot himself. We've sent a doctor and an ambulance but it's a bit late for them to do anything."

Chapter 13

"It's worse than Piccadilly Circus in here," Bright complained as he fought his way through the hall. Two scene-of-crime officers were standing by the study door while a third took photographs of the room and the body from every conceivable angle. A constable was standing by the drawing-room door, keeping the family out of the way, and two more were awaiting orders. Bright went over to a sergeant from the Chelsea station who was busy talking to the police surgeon.

"What the hell happened?" he asked shortly.

The doctor looked at the sergeant, who in turn looked at his boots before answering, "The bare facts would seem to be that Richard Ellis was in the study, supposedly going over some papers from work. He was on his own. Our constable was standing on the doorstep when he heard the shot. It took him a few seconds to open the door and, as he entered the hall, he saw Miss Swainson go into the study and heard her scream. Mr David Ellis was running down the stairs and Lady Ellis opened the drawing-room door at that moment. The constable rushed into the study, where he saw Richard lying on the floor. Miss Swainson was sitting, cradling his head in her lap, or rather, she was cradling what was left of his head in her lap. There was a gun, loosely held in Richard's right hand. From preliminary examination of the scene, it would appear that he had been sitting in the chair by the desk, put the gun to his right temple and shot himself. He was lying slightly to the left of the chair as if he had fallen out of it with the force of the shot. Miss Swainson was too hysterical to question properly, but it appeared that she had been making everyone a cup of coffee. She had just reached the top of the stairs up from the kitchen when she heard the shot. As you can see, she dropped the tray of coffee there, rushed straight into the study and was the first to reach Richard."

"Any note?" Bright asked.

"Yes. It's a bit bloodstained and we haven't been able to touch it yet, but the SOCs have nearly finished. I took a quick look and I think it says, 'I killed him, I had to, but it hasn't worked out.' It isn't signed."

"Okay. Thanks a lot. Do you mind if I have a quick look at the scene and then perhaps go to see the rest of the family?"

"Sure, go right ahead. They are all in the drawing room. Miss Swainson's in a bit of a state but the doc says he won't give her anything until after you've seen her."

"Thanks."

Bright went slowly into the study, closely followed by Hoppy. The SOC officers were just finishing off collecting samples of blood from the stains on the furniture, the photographer having already taken shots of the spatter patterns. Richard's body lay grotesquely positioned and with little more than a bloody mess where the left side of his head should have been. In various bags were items that were being sent to forensics. There was a bloodstained handkerchief with the initials R.E. embroidered in the corner, the suicide note and the bullet, which had been found on the floor in an area liberally splattered with blood, brain and fragments of bone.

"Jesus!" said Bright. "If that's the sort of result you get from a piddly little gun like that, I would hate to see the damage something like a Magnum could cause."

There didn't seem to be much else of interest in the study, so Bright and Hoppy gladly left the morbid scene and went to interview what was left of the family.

* * *

In the drawing room, Bright found a small and shocked group, far more closely touched by this new development than they had ever been by Sir Edward's death.

Margaret was sitting hunched on the edge of her chair, compulsively wiping her bloodstained hands on a tea towel. She was wearing a dark-brown, patterned dress, but Bright could easily see the large, darker stain down the front. He decided not to question Margaret immediately – she was in no fit state to answer him.

"I'm sorry to have to intrude, but perhaps I could just ask a few questions?" Bright addressed a very pale and haggard Lady Ellis. She nodded and then went back to looking at the large, white handkerchief that she was holding in her hands.

"Did Richard seem at all upset this evening?"

"Yes, Inspector, he was absolutely panic-stricken," she said in a tired voice. "But you should know that. After all, he was acutely worried when he left you at the station. It's hardly surprising, considering that you had virtually accused him of murdering his father."

Bright cleared his throat. "Yes, right, Lady Ellis. Perhaps you could tell me about the gun. Is it the same one that I gave back to you after Sir Edward's death?"

"Yes, it is. I'm afraid I have only myself to blame for that. I couldn't think where it should go, so I put it back in the desk. I locked the drawer, but put the key back where it was usually kept. Richard would have had no difficulty laying his hands on it, especially as he had taken over Edward's study."

Margaret started to cry quietly. Bright stood up and said that he would ask the doctor to come in.

"I'll take Margaret upstairs," David said. "Perhaps you could ask the doctor to see her there?"

"Of course," Bright answered. He stood at the door as David helped Margaret out, but stopped him as he passed and asked quietly, "We'll need Miss Swainson's clothes if you could possibly let us have them, Mr Ellis?"

David paused momentarily before nodding and hurrying to catch up with his stepsister.

As Bright wandered back into the hall, Hoppy came over. "The press have arrived in force, guv. Looks like every major paper had someone monitoring police radio frequencies and they have each sent a couple of reporters plus a photographer. Mind you, they could all be psychic, I suppose."

"More like psycho than psychic, Hoppy. Are the Chelsea lot keeping them at bay all right?"

"Oh yes, but it's going to be a bit difficult coming and going."

At that moment the front door opened again and Naseby entered backwards. The constable on duty outside was holding back the reporters despite the flashes from the cameras, which were almost blinding him. Naseby shouted, "I really have nothing to say just at this moment," before he managed to close the door, leaving the constable to deal with the howling mob.

Naseby came straight over to Bright and asked him what had happened.

"We obviously don't have any forensic reports or anything like that yet, but it looks as though Richard rather terminally shot himself, having first written a suicide note confessing to the murder of his father."

Naseby listened intently as Bright told him and then shook his head in disbelief. "It seems hardly credible. I really can't believe it of Richard. He seemed too timid. I mean actually to kill his own father like that, albeit for a large amount of money. Of course, it was also to keep himself out of jail. Yes, somehow I think that must have been the real reason. It seems more likely." He nodded to himself, content to have found a satisfactory explanation. "How's the rest of the family taking it?" he asked.

"Not very well, particularly Miss Swainson. She was first on the scene and it has understandably shocked her."

"Poor girl, I can imagine. Well, I'd better go in and see Lady Ellis, unless there is anything I can do for you?"

"Yes, actually, there is one question you could answer for me," Bright admitted, and led Naseby away from everyone.

"It's just to satisfy my curiosity, of course, but I want to know who gets the money now?" Bright asked in a conspiratorial whisper.

"That, actually, is rather an interesting legal question," Naseby said enthusiastically. "You see it's well known that a murderer cannot benefit from his crime and neither can the murderer's heirs, technically. So, if Richard really did kill his father, then his inheritance is revoked, becomes part of the residue, and thus passes to Lady Ellis. However, David and Mrs Ellis, as Richard's two next of kin and therefore his heirs as he had not yet made a will, may choose to challenge the fact that Richard killed Sir Edward. There are several possible grounds for the challenge; they could say that he was insane, under duress, or even that he was in the habit of confessing to murders that he had not committed. If they did choose to challenge Richard's confession, it would have to go to court. However, in my opinion, as there is a note – tantamount to a deathbed confession, so to speak – it will carry considerable weight with the court. Deathbed confessions tend to be believed more than the ones the police extract on the whole. No offence, I hope. Anyway, I'd put my money on Lady Ellis getting Richard's inheritance. Now, if you don't mind, I'd better go and see the good lady." He turned and left a very thoughtful Bright.

"C'mon Hoppy, let's go on back to the station. There's not a lot we can do here. It's just a question of waiting for the forensic reports and we can do that from there.

* * *

Chief Superintendent Willard was very pleased with the way things had turned out.

"Very neat," he said. "Very neat indeed. Once we get confirmation from forensics, we can tell the press that as far as we are concerned the case is closed and leave the rest to their imagination." He snapped the file shut, stood up and rubbed his hands together. "Not quite the way we would have liked it to end. No one gets much in the way of credit but at least no one is up shit creek either." He looked directly at Bright as he said this. "And we can get the men back on the beat to investigate the backlog of burglaries and off all this overtime, which will be a great relief." He marched briskly out of the room, humming contentedly to himself.

Sergeant Harper was already dismantling the incident room. The maps were being removed from the wall, the desks were being taken back to their original offices and files were being stacked in the corridor. Bright wandered over to the window and stood staring out at the passers-by. It was a clear, crisp and frosty night, and his breath momentarily clouded the glass.

"What's up, guv?" Hoppy asked. "You don't seem too pleased with it all. Is it 'cos it's a bit of an anticlimax or are you upset that you aren't going to get a pat on the back and promotion?"

"I don't know, Hoppy. I don't think that is the problem. Whatever it is, though, I can't put my finger on it. Maybe it's just that the whole thing is too neat." He wiped his condensed breath from the window and watched a lady of the night, well wrapped against the cold, walking slowly down the well-lit street. No customers would be interested; she was in the wrong area at the wrong time, but no doubt she would learn from experience.

"I don't know what you're so unhappy about, guv. The case is cleared up and you are at least off the hook, so what are you worrying about?"

"I'm not worrying over nothing, Hoppy, honest I'm not. Look, you piss off home. There are one or two things I want to sort out here."

"Oh no, you don't. That's just not on, guv. If the case isn't finished then we'd better get a move on and sort it out before we're given something else to do."

Bright smiled. It was no less than he had expected, but it was still nice to know that Hoppy was always prepared to assist him.

"Thanks, Hoppy. Look, I got on to forensics and told them I was unhappy about things. I did a lot of arm twisting and they eventually agreed to work through the night to get the results."

"My God, that is a turn-up for the books. I ain't never heard of them agreeing to that even when a life depended on it."

"I must admit it wasn't easy, but when you are as charming as I am, Hoppy, nothing is impossible."

Hoppy snorted. "Charm, my arse," was all he said.

Bright smiled and continued, "I really think it's important that we know exactly what happened as soon as possible."

"I should have thought that it was pretty obvious what happened."

"Well maybe it's too obvious then, Hoppy." Bright pulled at his beard. "Where was everybody? We know the constable was outside the front door, Margaret was on her way up the stairs from the kitchen, David was somewhere upstairs and Lady Ellis was in the drawing room. Nobody was with anybody else and nobody could see if any of the others went into the study. It's all too neat, or too untidy, I'm not sure which."

"So, what do we do while we are waiting for those results to put your mind at rest?"

For a few moments Bright seemed undecided. At last, he picked up his jacket and slung it over his shoulder. "Sergeant Harper, could you arrange for those results to get to me at the Ellis's house?"

"Of course, sir," she said.

"C'mon then, Hoppy. I've got to go back and talk to them again. I want to know exactly where they all were when the shot was fired."

* * *

"I was just off to bed actually, Inspector," David explained as he showed them into the drawing room. "My stepmother and Margaret will already have gone to sleep. At least they should have; the doctor gave them some tablets to take. I saw them both safely upstairs and then went over to see Mum at her hotel. I thought I'd better tell her in person, it's not the sort of thing you can say on the telephone, but I got there to discover a policeman had already been there. She was very upset, as you can imagine. I wish now that I had telephoned her and warned her about it. It's just that I can't really believe it's happened." He slumped in an armchair and rubbed his eyes like a child.

"I'm sorry, sir, I know you must be tired but it is important. All I want is to know exactly where you were when you heard the shot this evening."

David hesitated for a moment before answering, "In my bedroom. It's at the top of the stairs, first door on the right."

"And you came down the stairs immediately you heard the shot?"

"Well, not immediately. You see, I was half undressed. I was running a bath in the bathroom just along the landing. I'd just taken off my trousers when I heard the shot, so it took me a couple of seconds to put them back on before I ran down the stairs."

"I see. So both you and the constable were delayed. Where were Lady Ellis and Miss Swainson when you came running down those stairs?"

"I heard the crash of the coffee tray that Margaret dropped at the top of the stairs before I had even come out of my bedroom. As I reached the bottom of the stairs, my stepmother opened the drawing-room door and Margaret was already in the study."

"What took her so long?" Bright asked.

"I'm sorry, Inspector? What took who so long?"

"Your stepmother. What took Lady Ellis so long to open the door? I mean Margaret was already in the study and you had time to put on your trousers before you came downstairs and your stepmother had only just made it to the drawing-room door. What took her so long?"

David thought for a moment and then shrugged. "I'm sorry, Inspector, but I don't know."

"I'm going to have to see her," Bright muttered to himself.

"I beg your pardon?" David asked politely.

"Your stepmother. I'm going to have to see her," he repeated. "Just for a moment or two, but I've got to ask her what took her so long, I'm afraid."

David nodded and pulled himself slowly out of the chair. "I'll go upstairs and wake her." When he reached the door, he turned to Bright. "I'll give you a call when you can come up." He seemed reluctant to disturb his stepmother but braced himself and left them. Hoppy visibly relaxed but Bright sat pulling at his beard and chewing his lower lip.

"Inspector!" David shouted in a panicky voice from the top of the stairs. "Come quickly!"

Bright and Hoppy leapt from the chairs and ran up to him. David had already returned to Lady Ellis's bedroom, where he was kneeling on the enormous and ancient four-poster. He was giving mouth-to-mouth resuscitation to a moribund and faintly blue Lady Ellis.

"Call an ambulance," David said urgently between breaths.

Hoppy went to the telephone on the bedside table and dialled 999. Bright took a surreptitious look around the room and then went for a closer look at the other bedside table. On it there was a half-empty glass of water, an empty bottle of sleeping tablets and a piece of folded-over notepaper and a pen. Very carefully, Bright picked up the paper and opened it, touching only the corners. The writing inside was so shaky that it was almost indecipherable. Bright peered at it, mouthing the words as he finally made them out.

"I'm so sleepy," the note said, "I can't think straight, my whole world is crumbling before my very eyes, and I no longer want to witness its destruction."

He folded the note again and replaced it. He could hear the sirens in the distance and went downstairs to warn the constable on the door. When the ambulance arrived, Bright sent the constable upstairs to make sure that nothing was moved unless it was absolutely necessary. As the back-up arrived Bright put them in the picture but held them back until the ambulance men had decided whether or not to move Lady Ellis to hospital. Margaret had woken with all the noise and was standing, barefoot and dazed, on the landing.

"What's happening? What's going on? Where are you taking Mummy?" she said as David busily helped the ambulance men to carry Lady Ellis down the stairs. They were trying to continue with the resuscitation, periodically squeezing a bag attached to the mask over her face. Hoppy took Margaret to one side and explained to her what was happening. Bright watched from the hall as Margaret at first seemed unable to understand, then suddenly rushed back into her room, slamming the door behind her. Hoppy came down to the hall and spoke to Bright.

"David's going to the hospital in the ambulance, in case he can be of any help," he said. "Margaret's getting dressed and I said we'd take her on to the hospital. She's in no fit state to drive herself."

"Okay, Hoppy. Once the SOC officers are here and start work, we can leave this wretched house safely in their hands and follow everyone else. I'm beginning to feel that we ought to make this whole bloody place a scene of crime and set up the office in the hospital."

Chapter 14

In the waiting area outside Casualty, the chairs were hard and Bright fidgeted with discomfort as he sipped a cup of instant tea from the vending machine.

"What the hell's going on in there?" he asked, standing and pacing up and down impatiently. He stopped and read several of the notices taped to the walls. "Did you know there was a disco tonight in the social club, and that the stoma therapist will be happy to visit anyone on the wards should they want to see her?" He chewed his lower lip and stuck his hands in his trousers pockets. "What in God's name has happened to those bloody forensic reports? You would have thought that they could at least have given me some kind of preliminary idea on what happened." He paced up and down a bit more. "You did let Sergeant Harper know where we were?"

"She'd gone home actually, guv, but I spoke to her relief, Greaves, and he promised to let us know as soon as they called. So stop worrying and drink your tea," Hoppy said.

"It's gone cold and it was pretty revolting when it was hot. How long is it since we got here?"

"Only a couple of hours, guv, and believe me that is only like a few seconds when compared to the average wait in a casualty department."

Bright sat down again, but very quickly jumped up again.

"There's signs of movement, Hoppy. Yes, it definitely looks as though they're going to move Lady Ellis somewhere else. At least the sheet's not over her head, so she can't be going to the morgue."

They watched as two porters quickly pushed the trolley along the corridor. There was a doctor and two nurses, all wearing theatre dress, in attendance. The nurses' prime concern seemed to be to take care of the tubes and other items of equipment attached to their patient. The doctor was only interested in the portable ventilating machine attached to a tube coming from Lady Ellis's mouth. David and Margaret followed well to the rear.

Bright and Hoppy ran along the maze of underground corridors at a respectful distance, but were left behind when Lady Ellis and her entourage went up in the lift. They waited until they knew which floor she was being taken to and then went up in the second lift. They emerged on the fifth floor of the new block but had no idea where to go next. There was a large sign over the main ward entrance saying:

> Intensive Care Unit
> No unauthorised admittance
> Please ring bell

But Bright was reluctant to do so because everyone inside looked very busy. All the staff seemed to be wearing theatre outfits rather than the traditional uniforms worn by the nurses in the rest of the hospital. They all seemed to have masks and stethoscopes hung around their necks as well.

"How on earth are you supposed to know who's in charge or even who are the doctors and who are the nurses?" Bright asked Hoppy as he watched them from the door.

"I suppose if I were to say that the doctors are the male ones and the nurses are the female ones, you'd say that I was being old-fashioned and sexist to boot."

Bright just grunted.

At last, David and Margaret came out of a room and sat on some chairs in the corridor. Margaret seemed very distressed, looking grey, tired and shocked, but David was more in control. He put his arm around her, gave her a reassuring hug and then looked up. Seeing Bright and Hoppy still patiently waiting, he came over to talk to them.

"How is she?" Bright asked, nodding in the general direction of the ward.

"They can't really say anything for certain at this stage, but they certainly haven't written her off. The pills have produced unconsciousness and respiratory failure, which is why she is on a ventilator, but if they can just keep her going until her body metabolises the drugs, she should regain consciousness and breathe for herself again. Once she has pulled through the initial coma, they will be able to assess what permanent brain, liver or kidney damage there is, if any." David stopped and rubbed his face with the palms of his hands. "It's been a long night, but I keep trying to think about the medical problems, anything rather than think about what's happened in the last twenty-four hours. It's too much, it hasn't even begun to sink in." Once again he paused. Bright noticed that his eyes were red-rimmed as he turned to look at Margaret again.

"They're just sorting out my stepmother, you know, getting her onto the main ventilators and everything, and then Margaret and I will be able to go and sit with her for a while. Margaret wants to stay with her but as there really isn't anything we can do except get in the way, I'm going to go home and try to get some sleep. I feel that if I get some rest, I might be able to make some sense out of all this. I've tried to persuade Margaret to come home but she insists on staying." David wandered tiredly back to Margaret and sat down next to her.

Hoppy looked at Bright, curious as to why he seemed to have nothing to say. The inspector was busy playing with his beard and it was several minutes before he spoke.

"Hoppy, can you arrange to have a constable stay with Lady Ellis constantly? And you stay with her until the constable arrives. Tell the doctors that she's in protective custody or under arrest, or say that you have to stay near in case she comes round and says something. I don't care what, but don't get fobbed off with a chair outside the room. I want you to sit next to her."

"Okay, guv, I'll see to that. What are you up to?"

"I'm going to sort this out once and for all, Hoppy. I know it's the middle of the night, but I want this case well and truly over by the morning. I'm going to get those forensic reports and I want to speak to the scene-of-crime officers for a start. I'll keep the station informed as to where I am, so you can get in touch when you've got this end sorted."

"Right, guv," Hoppy acknowledged and watched as Bright left, brisk and determined to finish the business.

* * *

It was several hours later and dawn was breaking before he and Hoppy met up again as they arrived at the Ellises' family home in Chelsea. Hoppy had brought two uniformed constables with him, as requested by Bright on the telephone. He already knew that David and Margaret were at home and expecting him, and he had collected Mrs Ellis on the way. She was very pale and almost looked her age as he ushered her into the drawing room. He fussed around, making sure that everyone was sitting comfortably and that Hoppy was ready to make any notes that might be necessary. The two constables stood ready on either side of the door.

When everybody was settled and waiting nervously and expectantly for something to happen, Bright went and stood in front of the magnificent fireplace and prepared to lecture his audience.

"I've brought you all here together because I think that the time has come to end this case. From the beginning I've had problems with people not telling the truth. First we had the hospital staff trying to cover up their indiscretions and there was David being unhelpful as well, but we managed to sort all that out. But we still haven't got the whole truth and that is why I've come back again tonight, or rather this morning." He paused for a moment and looked at three of them. Only Margaret refused to meet his eye.

"You see, we were left with Richard, Lady Ellis, Mrs Ellis and Margaret, none of whom had alibis for Sir Edward's murder. Lady Ellis, Mrs Ellis and Margaret were also, most certainly, in the hospital on the night of the murder, and quite possibly at the actual time of the murder. We couldn't prove whether or not Richard had been there. Lady Ellis and Richard both had strong motives for killing Sir Edward, whereas Margaret and Mrs Ellis appeared to have little to gain. Richard was certainly the most likely person to have been mistaken for Dr Cawthorne, but it was not inconceivable, given the very dim lighting, for any of the others to have been mistaken for him as well. Margaret, Richard and Lady Ellis all had ample opportunity to steal the syringe from their own doctor's surgery. My main problem with that aspect of the case is that no one could have possibly known that they would be able to kill Sir Edward in that way until the day before his death, and no one visited the doctor in that period. So you see just how confusing that aspect of the case has been. As we obviously can't ask either Lady Ellis or Richard about their movements on the night of the murder, perhaps, Mrs Ellis, you and Margaret could explain what you were doing at the hospital on that night?"

Margaret jumped up and paced up and down angrily.

"Look, I've told you. Someone's made a mistake. I was never at the hospital that night, or any other night, for that matter. I didn't know and I didn't care which ward my stepfather was in and I certainly didn't visit him. I mean, Inspector, Richard has confessed to murdering his father, so why are you still asking questions about it? It just doesn't make sense."

"Let's just say I'm doing it to satisfy my curiosity, okay?" Bright was tired and more than a little ragged around the edges, but he was working hard at keeping calm. Margaret flopped back into her seat and rested her head in her hands.

"I'm sorry, Inspector, it's just that I'm very much on edge and so tired I don't quite know what to do with myself."

David came over and put his arm around her, giving Bright a fierce look. "I'm sure the inspector understands, Margaret," he said pointedly.

Bright held up both hands in surrender. "Perhaps you wouldn't mind telling us what you were doing at the hospital, Mrs Ellis?"

The strain of the past few days was definitely showing and even in the dim lamplight, her face looked ravaged. "Yes, Inspector. I do believe that the time has come for us all to be straight with you. Perhaps if we had all been honest from the start, Richard might still be alive. As I already told you, Inspector, I was in the hospital that night. I did tell you the truth, but I did also omit to tell you why I was there. I went to the hospital to ask Edward to help with my medical bills." She sighed with relief. "There, I've told you all. I was on a begging mission. I had written to him to explain why I needed the money but he wrote back to say that if the French didn't have the treatment available and if I couldn't get it on the National Health Service either, then it obviously wasn't any good anyway. He couldn't understand how much it meant to me just to try it. I thought that I might be able to persuade him, if I saw him face to face, especially as he was ill himself. I couldn't do it, though. It wasn't fair to twist his arm when he was unwell, so I left again. There, now you know it all."

David left Margaret and went over to his mother. "I'll look into this treatment, Mum. If there's anything in it, we'll find a way of paying for it. Don't you worry about it." He gave her a hug. "You should have talked to me about it before. I can quite easily check if it's reputable."

"I don't think it really matters if it's reputable or not, dear, so long as I believe it may work." She smiled sadly and held on to David's hand for a second before sending him back to his seat.

"Thank you, Mrs Ellis," Bright responded. "That at least clears up one of our problems. Now, unless anyone else has anything to say?" He stared hard at Margaret, but she steadfastly refused to meet his eye. "Then we shall move on to Richard's suicide; that is when the murderer really ran into trouble. You see, our forensic services are not stupid and they get plenty of practice at looking into gunshot wounds and their associated scenes." He paused for effect. David was looking dumbfounded, Mrs Ellis just looked tired but interested and Margaret continued to stare into the dying embers of the fire. The room was growing cold and Bright wished that someone would throw on some more logs.

"Let me tell you about some of the things that were found at the scene of Richard's supposed suicide. Richard was shot at very close range – within half an inch of the skin, to be exact, which is quite consistent with suicide. His were the only fingerprints on the gun, but they were only found where he was actually holding the gun. So, how did he pick it up. Even if he picked it up by the butt straight away, the prints should be slightly smeared. It is impossible to pick up a gun straight away in the firing position unless it is handed to you, but in that case there should be more prints on the gun. It is possible that Richard used the handkerchief, which we found under the chair in the study, to pick up the gun, though why he should do so I can't imagine. And what about that handkerchief? It was embroidered with the initials R.E., so it presumably belonged to Richard. The only problem is that it was found too far from the body to have been dropped after the shot, and it was too heavily bloodstained to have been where it was found when the shot was fired. So, it must have been moved after the event. Does any of you, by any chance, remember moving it?" He looked first at David, who was busy trying to remember, and then at Margaret, who was just looking blank.

"No, I must say that I don't remember seeing a handkerchief at all," David finally answered. "How about you, Margaret?"

"I don't remember anything," said Margaret. She seemed on the verge of hysterics. "I can't think about it without seeing Richard's head. I can't stop seeing him lying there." She stopped as David rushed over and put his arm round her again.

"That's okay, Margaret, it's all right. It doesn't matter if you can't remember the handkerchief. You probably kicked it under the chair without noticing." He turned to Bright. "Can't this wait? I mean, you can see that she's in no fit state to answer questions; it really isn't right."

"Murder isn't right either, Mr Ellis, and I really feel it is important to ask these questions here and now, rather than down at the station later."

David grudgingly nodded for Bright to continue but stayed with Margaret, sitting on the arm of her chair to give her moral support.

"We tested the handkerchief for cordite and the reaction was so strong that it looks as though whoever shot Richard used the handkerchief to hold the gun as he or she fired. They must then have put the gun in his hand and thrown the handkerchief down. It was a mistake to throw it so far away from the body. It aroused the suspicions of the scene-of-crime officers from the start. So you see, we can be pretty certain that Richard did not commit suicide, and that means that he was murdered."

"What about the note? The other sergeant said it was almost definitely in Richard's own handwriting," David queried.

"Yes, it looks like it. Of course we don't have the final graphology results yet and I might be proved wrong, but I think that Richard must have been forced to write the note before he was shot."

There was a short silence as they all thought about the full implications of what Bright had been saying.

David shook his head, unable to believe it all. "So what's the idea then, Inspector?" he asked. "You can't seriously believe that my stepmother nipped into the study, forced Richard to write a suicide note, shot him, put the gun into his hand, rushed out of the room and quickly hid in the drawing room, all in a matter of a few seconds before Margaret arrived on the scene with the coffee tray, can you? I mean, Margaret didn't even see the drawing-room door closing."

"Wait a minute," Margaret interrupted. "You are wrong. I did see the drawing-room door closing as I came up the stairs, now that you mention it. I'd just heard the shot, came running up, saw the door closing and then dropped the tray as I ran across the hall to see Richard."

Bright nodded and said, "There you are, you see? And it would also explain what took her so long to come out after hearing the shot. It probably took her a few seconds to catch her breath after all that rushing about."

"God," David said in exasperation. "I just can't believe it. And what about her own suicide attempt? Was that kosher?"

Bright shrugged. "We're still waiting for a scene-of-crime report and for the forensic reports; until I have those I can't really comment."

"It's just incredible. I mean I can understand her killing Dad – after all, it was hardly unprovoked – but Richard? Never. Richard never harmed her intentionally. To kill him was cowardly and I would never have described her as that." David seemed quite convinced that he was right.

"Maybe she needed the money." Bright put forward this theory tentatively, and it was Mrs Ellis who replied.

"No, Inspector, David is right. The killing of Edward was a positive and brave act to protect herself, her child and also her stepchildren. But the killing of Richard was very different indeed. She would never have done it."

The telephone started to ring in the hall and Bright went to answer it. He was out of the room for several minutes and when he returned, he seemed surprised by the news he had heard.

"That was the scene-of-crime bloke from Chelsea with some news for me and he had some more of the forensic reports as well." He stopped for a moment, rubbed his beard and pulled a face at Hoppy. Then he turned. "Miss Swainson, I have to say that I am placing you under arrest and I must caution you that you have the right to remain silent but that anything you do say will be written down and may be used in evidence at your trial."

"What on earth are you doing, Inspector?" David asked as he stood up. Mrs Ellis nodded as if everything now made sense.

Margaret stared silently at Bright. "I think that I shall remain silent at least until I have spoken to Mr Naseby," she finally said.

"As you wish," Bright answered. David, obviously glad of something to do, hurried out to telephone him. Bright said nothing while David was in the hall and even when he returned and reported that Naseby was leaving immediately, the silence continued. Bright looked at his watch several times as the minutes passed and then suddenly stood up.

"Right, well, I think that we should adjourn to the station. If you would just fetch your coat or whatever you need, Miss Swainson?"

Margaret left to find her things and Bright nodded for one of the constables by the door to accompany her. David rushed out to try and reach Naseby and tell him to go straight to the police station, but he had already left. Bright had timed it perfectly.

* * *

The interview room smelled rather less of urine and more of disinfectant but had not changed in any other way. Margaret was sitting tense and rigid in the hard, upright chair and a WPC, silent, aloof and strangely menacing, stood by the door.

Outside, Bright had a quick word with Hoppy. "I'd like to have left her to sweat a bit, but we don't have long before Naseby arrives and starts to throw his weight around. So, we'll have to go in and hit her hard. We'll do the usual routine."

He led the way in to the room and asked the WPC to sit at the table and take the contemporaneous interview notes. Since the PACE Act, every single word that was said by anyone in the room during the interview had to be written down in longhand and each page signed as correct.

"Miss Swainson," Bright began, "I thought you might like to hear some of the evidence we have against you. Probably the most significant is the report on the blood-spatter patterns on your dress. They show conclusively that you must have been standing less than three feet from Richard when the shot was fired. Perhaps you would like to comment on that?"

Margaret remained silent but she had become strangely still as she stared at the bare wall behind Bright.

"The scene-of-crime officers also report that in a full and sealed black plastic rubbish bag, which had been placed outside the back door, they found the outer shells of about thirty capsules of the type of hypnotic sleep inducer used by Lady Ellis. It seems unlikely that she would have bothered to do that for herself, and even if she did, why would she try to conceal them? It suggests the possibility of someone having given her the contents of those capsules dissolved in a drink. Coincidentally, there was a cup newly washed up, in the kitchen, and it had your fingerprints all over it."

Margaret didn't even bother to look at Bright as she answered him in a flat and emotionless voice, "I came downstairs and had a cup of milk because I couldn't sleep. I rinsed it out and left it to drain."

"That certainly explains the cup, Miss Swainson. I just wonder what exactly we shall find from the analysis of Lady Ellis's stomach contents."

Bright was bluffing. By the time Lady Ellis had arrived at the hospital and had had her stomach pumped out, there was only a small amount left, probably not enough for them to be certain that she hadn't taken the pills with the water by her bed. He hoped that Margaret wasn't aware of that and was gratified to see that she was looking worried.

"What was it like, eh? Watching your own mother having her stomach pumped and tubes being forced down her throat, in her arms and God knows where else?"

Margaret was still staring silently at the wall behind Bright but a tear slowly trickled down her face.

"Perhaps you enjoyed it, did you? Did you like watching your own mother being cruelly abused and thrown about? Or were you too worried that she might survive? Because she might, you know, she might regain consciousness and tell us what happened. She might tell us how you made her a drink. How do you think she is going to feel, knowing that her own daughter tried to kill her? Even if she recovers from the coma, you may still have succeeded. You may have to watch her die, slowly and painfully, from liver or kidney failure. Are you prepared for that?"

"Stop it! Stop it! I can't stand it. I can't listen to you going on about it anymore," Margaret sobbed and put her hands over her ears, but Bright came around the desk and pulled them away.

"You're going to listen to this, Miss Swainson, every sordid and gory detail. You've killed twice, quite possibly three times, and I'm not going to spare you anything." He spoke quietly with his face very close to hers, and then returned to his seat. He waited for a few moments, until her sobs had degenerated into irregular hiccups and the WPC had caught up.

"Why did you do it? Couldn't you wait to get your hands on the money? Or did you just get into the swing of killing and then couldn't stop?"

"No, it wasn't like that," she cried, but then once again refused to say more. She sat, shaking her head vigorously, trying not to listen to Bright's persistent questions.

"What was it like? Did she guess that you were involved? Did she threaten you? You must have had a pretty good reason to kill your own mother, or was it something Freudian, Jungian or whatever? Come on, don't piss us about, we know you did it, but why?" And he thumped the table with his clenched fist.

After a short pause, Hoppy stepped forward and put his arm around her shoulders.

"You might as well make it easy on yourself, love. I mean, we know you did it, we can prove it, and it will look better in court if you co-operated with us. What was she going to do? Cut you off without a penny? Turn you in? Pretty ungrateful of her considering she benefited from Sir Edward's death even more than you did."

Margaret nodded. "She didn't understand."

"I don't suppose she bloody well did!" Bright cut in sharply. "After all, you killed her husband and her stepson.

She was probably asking herself who was next in line for the chop!"

"I had to stop her," Margaret burst out.

"I'm sure you did," Hoppy said comfortingly. "Going to turn you in, was she?"

Margaret shook her head and blew her nose. "She wouldn't have done that, but she was going to change her will. She was going to write a letter and give it to Naseby. He was to open it in the event of her death, if it was suspicious, or if I ever challenged her new will. I had to stop her before she saw Naseby. I'm so tired. When will I be able to get some sleep?"

"Just as soon as you've made a full statement, Miss Swainson."

She nodded tiredly. "When I saw her in Intensive Care, with all those tubes and the machine breathing for her, I knew then. I knew that I had done wrong. I knew that I would have to pay for it all."

"Where did you get the syringe?" Hoppy coaxed.

"I'd had it for years. I got it from a doctor, the father of one of my school friends. We used to have water-pistol fights using the syringes and I'd kept one as a sort of memento of happier times. I'd completely forgotten about it until Mummy came home and told me about all the drips and things. I remembered an old television programme where someone used a syringe to kill and the idea slowly grew on me." She seemed cold, almost detached from what she was saying.

"Did you wear gloves?"

She nodded. "I took the rubber ones from the kitchen." She was silent for a moment and then burst out, "I didn't mean to kill anyone else, but I had to give you a murderer to get you off my back and Richard was the perfect scapegoat because you already suspected him."

"Why did you drop the tray?"

"I didn't. I put it at the top of the stairs, killed Richard and then kicked it as I ran back to make it sound as though I had dropped it when I heard the shot."

"How did you manage to delay your mother? Did you jam the door?"

She nodded and murmured, "With the rug."

"What about Richard? How did you get him to write the note?"

She stared silently at her hands.

"How did you get him to do it? Did you threaten to kill him if he didn't?"

She nodded again.

"And you killed him when he did." Bright was tired. He slumped in his chair and it was a few seconds before he realised that Margaret was quietly speaking again.

"Half his head was missing. I felt really sick when I saw it in my lap. On the television the wound always seems so small, just a tiny hole with a trickle of blood, but there were bits of Richard's head all over the wall. Oh God," she sobbed.

Epilogue

It was several days before Lady Ellis was considered well enough to see Bright. As he went into the intensive care unit, he was shocked at how old and haggard she looked in the harsh, fluorescent light. As he sat down, she indicated that he should move closer. The endotracheal tube that had been used to ventilate her had bruised her vocal cords and she could only whisper hoarsely. There was noise all around them, nurses rushing from one place to another, their sandals clattering on the polished lino, monitors blipping, ventilators hissing, and Bright had great difficulty hearing what she had to say.

"I blame myself for what she did, Inspector. You see, she killed Edward because she sensed that I wanted him dead. I really believed that he would die when he was taken ill. I believed that God was stopping him from deserting us, taking all his money and sending my brother, his own son and all the others to jail. I was so disappointed when he survived the operation and that was what made Margaret decide to kill him." She fell back on her pillows, exhausted by the effort needed to talk. Bright sat silently, waiting for her to regain her breath.

"She killed Edward for me. She killed Richard out of fear," she continued. "She was wrong to do that and I'm sure that she realises that but, when even I turned on her, she attacked me. She was a cornered and wounded animal and she acted instinctively. Is there nothing I can do to help her?"

Bright was sure that Naseby would have already told her that, with Margaret's confession, the only way she could help was to be a character witness at the trial, but as he shook his head he saw the faint glimmer of desperate hope he had seen in her eyes dim. She closed her eyes and waved her hand vaguely in dismissal. Bright wondered if she would feel better or worse when she discovered that Margaret had killed Sir Edward for money rather than for her. It was difficult to tell how she would take it.

"There's just one more thing, Lady Ellis. Were you in the hospital on the night Sir Edward was murdered?"

"Yes, yes. I did make that phone call internally. I was coming to ask Edward once more to reconsider. I telephoned the ward from a phone in the nurses' home and I could see the television in their sitting room as I talked. The nurse told me that Edward was asleep, so I decided not to see him and went home. It's quite simple really and I should have told you from the start, but it seemed to complicate things unnecessarily. I wanted to persuade Edward not to incriminate Lionel with the Fraud Squad." She smiled weakly. "It seems such a long time ago now."

As he walked along the corridors, he felt depressed. The case had finished well for him, but a whole family had been shattered by it. A father and son dead, a young girl in jail, and now that the Fraud Squad were investigating Lionel Woods it looked as though he might end up inside for a while, too. Lady Ellis was left very much on her own and there was little she could do about it.

To cheer himself up, Bright went in search of Fiona. He could rely upon her to blow away his cobwebs and banish his blues. At the main gate, he was surprised to see Mrs Ellis half hidden behind an enormous bunch of vivid flowers. She was asking the way to Intensive Care, hoping to see Lady Ellis. Bright smiled as he thought that perhaps she wouldn't be so entirely alone, after all.

THE END

The Book Folks & Joffe Books Story

The Book Folks began in 2013, founded by Erik Empson with a simple but powerful goal — to publish highly readable, compelling fiction that readers would love. With a focus on crime fiction, thrillers and gripping mysteries, The Book Folks quickly built a loyal audience and became known for championing talented authors from the UK, Ireland, the US and beyond.

From gritty police procedurals and psychological thrillers to fast-paced action and suspense, The Book Folks earned a reputation for curating addictive stories at affordable prices — often introducing readers to hidden gems and breakout talent.

In 2025, The Book Folks proudly became part of Joffe Books, the UK's largest independent publisher. Joffe Books started in 2014 when Jasper Joffe published his mum's long-rejected romance novel — which unexpectedly became a bestseller. That spirit of risk-taking and reader-first publishing has defined Joffe Books ever since.

Together, Joffe Books and The Book Folks are united by a passion for page-turning fiction and a deep respect for the authors who create it. We're proud to publish some of the best-loved names in fiction — including Joy Ellis, Faith Martin, Caro Ramsay, Simon Brett, Helen Forrester, and Robert Goddard — as well as fresh voices bringing new energy to the genre.

We never forget that everything begins with the author's story — and that continues with you, the reader.

We love hearing from you, so get in touch any time at feedback@joffebooks.com.

And if you'd like to receive free books and hear about our latest releases, sign up to our newsletter:
www.joffebooks.com/freebooks

Thanks for reading — and for being part of our story.

www.thebookfolks.com

Printed in Dunstable, United Kingdom

76369678R00122